Forced to Marry

Gytha, twisting her fingers, said:

"I have always been told that you have . . . sworn you will . . . never marry."

"That is true," Lord Locke said. "I have no intention of marrying."

He could not imagine where this conversation was leading.

Gytha made a sound which was almost a sob.

"There is no way I can . . . prevent being forced to . . . marry unless you will . . . help me."

"What are you asking?" Lord Locke enquired.

Gytha took a deep breath.

"That . . . that you will . . . become . . . engaged to me!"

A Camfield Novel of Love
by Barbara Cartland

"Barbara Cartland's novels are all distinguished by their intelligence, good sense, and good nature."

—ROMANTIC TIMES

"Who could give better advice on how to keep your romance going strong than the world's most famous romance novelist, Barbara Cartland?"

—THE STAR

Camfield Place,
Hatfield
Hertfordshire,
England

Dearest Reader,

Camfield Novels of Love mark a very exciting era of my books with Jove. They have already published nearly two hundred of my titles since they became my first publisher in America, and now all my original paperback romances in the future will be published exclusively by them.

As you already know, Camfield Place in Hertfordshire is my home, which originally existed in 1275, but was rebuilt in 1867 by the grandfather of Beatrix Potter.

It was here in this lovely house, with the best view in the county, that she wrote *The Tale of Peter Rabbit*. Mr. McGregor's garden is exactly as she described it. The door in the wall that the fat little rabbit could not squeeze underneath and the goldfish pool where the white cat sat twitching its tail are still there.

I had Camfield Place blessed when I came here in 1950 and was so happy with my husband until he died, and now with my children and grandchildren, that I know the atmosphere is filled with love and we have all been very lucky.

It is easy here to write of love and I know you will enjoy the Camfield Novels of Love. Their plots are definitely exciting and the covers very romantic. They come to you, like all my books, with love.

Bless you,

CAMFIELD NOVELS OF LOVE
by Barbara Cartland

Other books by Barbara Cartland

A NEW CAMFIELD NOVEL OF LOVE BY

BARBARA CARTLAND

Forced to Marry

A JOVE BOOK

FORCED TO MARRY

A Jove Book/published by arrangement with
the author

PRINTING HISTORY
Jove edition/June 1987

ISBN: 0-515-09006-9

Jove Books are published by The Berkley Publishing Group,
200 Madison Avenue, New York, NY 10016.
The words "A JOVE BOOK" and the "J" with sunburst
are trademarks belonging to Jove Publications, Inc.

PRINTED IN THE UNITED STATES OF AMERICA

AUTHOR'S NOTE

The Viper is in a general sense any venomous snake and is usually restricted to members of the family of Viperidae. These are found in Europe, Asia, and Africa. The ten genera vary greatly in size and are of danger to man. Some have prehensile tails and are arboreal. Others are called mole snakes and are burrowers.

All these snakes can swim if necessary, and some species frequent the banks of streams and lakes. Their venom is introduced at the base of the fang and discharged into the wound. The quantity of venom and the depth of penetration vary with the size of the snake, and some small species are extremely dangerous.

All the dangerously venomous snakes in Europe are vipers of the Genus Vipera. The best known is the Common Viper and is the only venomous snake found in Great Britain.

chapter one

1818

"No, Grandpapa, it is absolutely impossible! I cannot do it!"

"You will do as I say," Sir Robert Sullivan roared. "If you think I am going to allow my money to be squandered by some smarmy fortune-hunter, you are very much mistaken!"

"Not every man who approaches me need be a fortune-hunter," Gytha said quietly.

"Do you think anyone would marry you for anything else?" Sir Robert retorted. "I am having no more arguments. You have your choice. You can marry Vincent or Jonathan, whichever you like, and the sooner the better."

With that he signalled to his valet, who was standing behind his wheelchair, and he was taken from the room.

Gytha watched him go, then sank down on the sofa.

"What can I . . . do?" she asked despairingly. "What can I . . . do?"

It seemed incredible, but she had realised in the last two months that her grandfather was deeply concerned about the disposal of his huge fortune.

The doctors had told Gytha privately it was unlikely he would live more than two or at the outside three months.

She had not repeated their confidential report to anyone.

But with what was often the uncanny perception of the old, Sir Robert was aware that his days were numbered.

He had often discussed the question of who would inherit his fortune, which he had accumulated in India during the last century.

No one knew exactly how much he owned except himself, his solicitor, and his accountant.

The few remaining members of his family were very conscious that it was an enormous sum.

Gytha knew that his two nephews, Vincent and Jonathan, the sons of his younger brother, were counting the days until they could inherit his wealth.

Sir Robert had been unfortunate in that he had only one son of his marriage.

He was killed at the Battle of Waterloo, before which he had produced just one daughter, Gytha.

Alex Sullivan was an exceptionally charming man who had enjoyed life enormously.

He had proved himself an outstanding leader in Wellington's Army.

When he was killed it had been a tragedy not only for his Regiment but also for his father.

He had relied on him to carry on the Sullivan name and ambitions.

Gytha had often thought that her father was not particularly interested in money.

He enjoyed being with people and found his pleasures in far more simple things than striving for wealth.

Her mother had been the same.

Coming from a County family, she loved the country.

She had no wish to go to London and appear at Balls, the Assemblies and the Receptions.

These continued to be given, glamorous and luxurious as ever, all through the war.

Instead, when her husband's Regiment left for Belgium, she had moved from the smaller house they occupied on the estate.

The huge mansion which her father-in-law, Sir Robert, had rebuilt and continually enlarged, became her home.

Sometimes she said laughingly to Gytha:

"I feel sometimes as if we are very small peas rattling in a very large pod!"

But after her husband, the charming Alex, had been killed, the great house seemed darker and more gloomy than ever.

It was almost as if she moved like a ghost among the huge, high-ceilinged rooms and up the enormous carved and gilt staircase.

Gradually Mrs. Sullivan seemed to loosen her hold on life and to fade away.

Gytha thought that it was not only the shock of her father's death.

It was that her mother could not believe it had really happened.

Soon she found herself alone with her grandfather.

Because he was getting very old, he offered no one any hospitality and she seldom saw anyone of her own age.

It was a miserable existence for any young girl.

Gytha found some solace in the horses that filled the big stables and which she thought were never exercised enough.

She used to ride every minute of the day she was not doing lessons with her Governesses.

They came and went in monotonous succession, for Sir Robert always found fault with them.

They either resented his interference, or found their existence so confining that they quickly looked for employment elsewhere.

Gytha, however, managed to teach herself very much better than they could do.

She was always in the enormous Library which was filled with books.

Many of the books had surprisingly only recently been published.

Her grandfather wished to be regarded as a well-read man.

He had always resented the fact that as a boy he had not been sent to one of the top Public Schools.

His one extravagance was to buy books.

Not only was his vast Library filled with them.

They overflowed into other rooms, where the estate-carpenter hastily provided shelves for them.

Books were, in fact, the one close contact Gytha managed to have with her grandfather.

When she went to see him after riding, she would quickly gloss over the fact that she had not been doing the lessons which he intended her to do.

Instead, she would begin telling him about some new book.

She found his mind was immediately diverted by what she could tell him about it.

Sometimes she would read aloud to him.

Mostly he preferred her to give him a synopsis in her own words of what she had read.

His eyes had grown weak.

He was unable to read for long and then only in a large print.

He therefore made Gytha into a story-teller.

Although she was not aware of it, this improved her English, her knowledge of Literature and the world, besides her elocution.

It was a strange life.

By the time she reached her eighteenth birthday, it was doubtful if any other girl had lived such a sheltered existence.

Unless the girl had been incarcerated in a Convent.

Then the blow had fallen.

Sir Robert suddenly realised that if he died soon, Gytha would be left alone.

Also if, as he intended, she inherited most of his wealth, fortune-hunters, like vultures, would descend on her.

She would not have the experience or the intelligence to cope with them.

The only possible alternative, he decided, was that she should marry one of her cousins.

They were the sons of his younger brother, Jason, whom he had never liked.

Actually he had not spoken to him for ten years before he was killed in a carriage accident.

Jason's sons, however, were too sensible not to realise where their interests lay.

They had then proceeded during the last six months to be constant visitors at the Hall.

Gytha, somewhat to her surprise, found herself disliking them both.

Vincent was, she supposed, a Buck when he was in London.

He affected the fashionable drawl which she found

not only irritating but it also made her feel small and insignificant.

He was thirty-five years of age and very much a "man about town."

Vincent set himself to make her aware of his importance in the social life in London.

Also his irresistible attraction for the "Fair Sex."

His valet, who was greatly disliked by the elderly servants in the Hall, boasted continually about his master's love-affairs with the most beautiful women in London.

The maids then relayed to Gytha everything he had said.

They had all known her since she was a child.

Consequently they were more outspoken than they would have been if they had not forgotten that she was now grown-up.

"If you ask me," one of them said to Gytha, "it ain't anything to boast about that you've broken some poor lady's heart! I couldn't see your father, God rest his soul, behaving in such a manner."

"No, indeed," Gytha agreed, "Papa would never have behaved like that!"

She disliked her Cousin Jonathan even more than his brother.

Vincent was condescending and obviously contemptuous of a girl who knew nothing of the world in which he shone.

She was sure he considered her dowdy and unattractive.

Jonathan, however, was a toady.

She watched him sucking up to her grandfather.

He did it so obviously and obsequiously that she felt embarrassed even to look at or listen to him.

When they first came to the Hall after her father's death, they paid her no attention.

In their eyes she was only a child.

They assumed also that Sir Robert would leave her, being a female, a small share of his money.

Perhaps he would leave enough to constitute a reasonable dowry.

The rest would go to them, because their name was Sullivan.

It was only in the last six months that they had grown suspicious.

Now, instead of more or less ignoring Gytha, Jonathan fawned on her.

Vincent paid her a few quite obviously insincere compliments.

Gytha was scornfully aware of what they were thinking.

Finally, after they had both returned to London, her grandfather had announced that he intended to make her his heir.

She had stared at him in astonishment.

"But you cannot do that, Grandpapa!"

"Who is to stop me?" the old man growled. "You need money and who I give it to is my affair. While I have no liking for either of my nephews, they are Sullivans and perhaps, if you have any sense in that head of yours, you will be able to improve them in one way or another."

"But Grandpapa . . . I could not contemplate marrying . . . either Vincent or Jonathan!"

"You will do as I tell you!" her grandfather shouted.

After that the same argument was repeated day after day.

The only fortunate thing about it was that neither

Vincent nor Jonathan knew about it.

They did not guess that her grandfather had finally made up his mind as to who should be his heir.

Now the altercation had flared up even more intensely because he had told her he had sent for both his nephews.

He expected them to arrive in two days time.

Gytha felt as if she were caught in a trap from which there was no escape.

It was impossible to think clearly in the house.

After her grandfather had left her for his own room, she jumped up and ran into the hall.

Picking up a thick coat she had left lying on one of the chairs, she put it on before a footman could help her.

"Yer going out, Miss Gytha?" he asked.

"I am going to the stables, Harry," Gytha replied. "If Grandpa asks for me, say you do not know where I am."

Harry, who had been at the Hall for some years, grinned.

"Yer can trust I, Miss."

Gytha was too perturbed to smile back at him.

She merely waited impatiently while he opened the front-door.

She stepped out into the cold air, which had intensified since the sun had set.

It made her feel it was something she needed at this particular moment.

She ran across the gravel courtyard to where on the left of the house there was a large archway.

It led into the stables.

The horses had already been shut up for the night, but she opened the stable door.

The animals she loved so much were all in their comfortable stalls.

They were either eating at the manger or already lying down on the fresh straw.

Abbey, the Head Groom, was most particular in having it changed every day.

Gytha opened the stall of one of her favourite horses, Dragonfly.

As she patted him and he nuzzled his nose affectionately against her, she said:

"Oh, Dragonfly, what am I to do? Help me because there is . . . no one else and I cannot and will not . . . marry someone I do not . . . love."

She thought as she spoke how supremely happy her father and mother had been together.

When her father had been killed, it was as if the light had gone out in her mother's world.

There was only darkness.

"I want to love . . . someone like that . . . Dragonfly," Gytha murmured.

As the horse twitched his ears, she knew he was listening and thought he understood.

Then she heard footsteps in the passage outside the stall.

It was Hawkins, who had been her father's batman.

He had come with her and her mother to the Big House when the war was over.

"I hears yer here, Miss," Hawkins said, "an' I comes to see if there be anythin' I can do for yer."

Hawkins had known Gytha ever since she was ten years old.

He was well aware that when she was upset, she always turned to the horses for comfort.

For the moment, however, she could not speak even to Hawkins of what she was feeling.

But she was certain that the valet who pushed her grandfather in his wheelchair would talk.

The whole household would already be aware what had occurred to upset her.

Hawkins came into the stall, and seeing the tears in Gytha's eyes, said:

"Now, don't you go upsettin' yerself, Miss Gytha. I was awaitin' to tell yer, there's a treat in store for us tomorrow."

"What is that?" Gytha managed to ask.

She was thinking as she did so that Vincent and Jonathan might be arriving tomorrow afternoon.

There would certainly be no treat in that.

"I happens to know," Hawkins replied, "there's a Steeple-chase taking place next door on His Lordship's estate. If us slip away in the mornin', we'd have a good view of it."

Gytha was instantly interested.

"A Steeple-chase, Hawkins? Do you mean to say His Lordship is back? I thought he was abroad."

"They tells I he's come 'ome," Hawkins said, "an' the first thing 'e arranges be a Steeple-chase with 'is friends acomin' down from London with th' finest horses as have ever been seen in these 'ere parts."

"Oh, Hawkins! Who told you all this?"

"I only hears about it today, Miss," Hawkins replied. "When I goes down t' the Green Man one o' the grooms from Locke Hall comes in for a pint o' ale."

He paused, and seeing Gytha's interest, went on:

"Talking big, 'e be, about the parties 'is Lordship's been givin' in London and now the Park'll be full of them Corinthians and th' stables overflowing."

Gytha laughed.

"Oh, Hawkins, how exciting! And of course we must go to watch the Steeple-chase! But do not say anything to the rest of the household, or that nasty valet of Grandpapa's will tell him what I am doing and he will make me stay at home."

"I wouldna tell that man th' time o' day if I could help it!"

Gytha laughed again.

She knew of the bitter feud between her grandfather's valet, who had been with him for years, and the rest of the staff.

They thought, and quite rightly, that he was a spy.

He did repeat to his Master everything that was said and done.

"What we will do, Hawkins," Gytha said, "is say we are just going for a short ride, as we usually do, and will be back for luncheon."

She looked at him as she added:

"But we may have to go hungry, unless you can get some sandwiches out of Cook without her knowing the reason why you want them."

"Yer leave it to me, Miss Gytha," Hawkins replied. "An' I don't mind bettin' yer 'is Lordship'll win the Steeple-chase an' no doubt about it."

"I expect he will," Gytha agreed, "and it will be lovely to see him riding again. I wonder if he has altered much in the last two years?"

"Got older," Hawkins said, "but th' groom at th' Green Man were aboasting that 'e went round th' course an' cleared every fence with a foot to spare!"

Gytha gave a little sigh of pleasure.

She remembered the last time she had seen Lord Locke out hunting.

She had thought then that no man could ride more magnificently.

He looked as if he were part of the horse he rode.

Although Lord Locke's estate marched with that of her grandfather, she had never met him.

Nor had he ever set foot inside the Hall.

This was due to a long-standing and bitterly waged war over a boundary wood.

Lord Locke's father had claimed it belonged to him, while Sir Robert had asserted it was his.

Both gentlemen raged at each other.

Then they summoned their Solicitors, who consulted ancient maps.

But they found no satisfactory answer to the question.

It ended with them snarling at each other like dogs and refusing to meet.

Even when it concerned County interests.

Lord Locke's family had lived at Locke Hall for several generations longer than the Sullivans had been in the County.

He was patron of the Horse-Show and of several commendable charities.

Sir Robert was patron of the Agricultural Show and a supporter of other local charities.

Their neighbours had preferred Lord Locke to Sir Robert.

Although there were a number who contrived to make themselves pleasant to both the elderly gentlemen.

Inevitably they fell between two stools.

When the present Lord Locke inherited, he had already distinguished himself as a soldier.

When hostilities were over, he became one of the

most admired and sought after young men in the *Beau Monde*.

He was outstanding as a horseman, which made him automatically a Corinthian.

He was an acclaimed pupil of Gentleman Jackson's Academy in Bond Street.

He was also a swordsman who, it was said, had defeated two of the European champions.

He was an undisputed expert whether with a gun at game-birds or with a pistol in a duel.

The stories about him were of course repeated and re-repeated by the employees on both his estate and Sir Robert's.

Gytha had thought of him as a hero ever since she could remember.

The sad thing was that she had never met him.

She had, however, seen him, which had been enough to stir her imagination and make him part of her dreams.

That after the war he should have chosen to journey round the world was, she thought, exactly what she might have expected him to do.

Rather than spend his time going from one beautiful woman's Boudoir to another's.

In fact, the story she heard from the country people was that he had no intention of getting married.

He wished to remain a bachelor for many years.

This merely added to the aura that surrounded him in her imagination.

She could never picture Lord Locke running after money as her cousins were doing.

Or spending his time ingratiating himself with a disagreeable old man like her grandfather just to get something out of him.

"Nothing will stop me from watching the Steeple-chase," she said to Hawkins. "We will go to the Rise by Monk's Wood, where it will be easy to see the whole course."

"I've heard as how 'is Lordship's altered it since he were here last."

"In what way?"

"He's extended it, made th' jumps higher an' more difficult."

"I wish I could jump them," Gytha said wistfully.

But she knew that however much she might watch and admire Lord Locke, it would be impossible for her ever to meet him.

The Steeple-chase had, however, swept away her misery and the horror of what her grandfather had planned for her.

When she went back to the house, she was smiling.

She no longer was thinking about herself, but about Lord Locke.

*   *   *

The next day, to Gytha's joy, the sky was clear.

The slight frost which had made the lawns white when she had first opened her window had cleared away in the sunshine.

She had no Governess at the moment.

The last one had been dispensed with by her grandfather on her eighteenth birthday.

There was fortunately no one to ask questions as to where she was going.

Her grandfather would not be down until nearly eleven o'clock.

It was therefore easy to hurry to the stables as soon as she had finished breakfast.

Hawkins was waiting for her.

She mounted Dragonfly and he was riding an equally fine horse by the name of Samson.

They set off, making it appear to the stable-lads and the Head Groom that they were heading for a short ride the way they usually went, with no other intentions in mind.

"Keep away from t' main roads, Miss Gytha," the Head Groom advised her just as she was moving off.

"Why?" she asked.

"There be a number o' carriages travelling to th' Hall, Miss."

"Then we will certainly do our best to avoid them," Gytha replied casually.

Only when they had ridden out of ear-shot did she see that Hawkins's eyes were twinkling.

He was a wiry, athletic little man, who was now getting on in years.

But her father had always said he would rather have him in a tight corner than anyone else he knew.

"What is more," her father had added, "there is nobody who can make me as comfortable as Hawkins, whether it means strangling a chicken for my dinner, or making me a bed in a pig-sty!"

Her mother had laughed. Then she said with a sob in her voice:

"Oh, darling, if only I could come to look after you! But I am afraid you would not want me to be a 'camp-follower.'"

"I like to think of you here, my precious," her father replied, "with all the things we have chosen together for our home. But I promise you, I will not stay away one minute longer if it is possible for me to return to you."

He had looked at her mother in a way which Gytha

knew was an expression of love without words.

Then they had moved into each other's arms.

Gytha had crept from the room knowing that for the moment they had forgotten her very existence.

But her father had never come back from the campaign.

Their house where he had been so happy was shut up.

Then there were only the large, gloomy empty rooms of the Hall and her grandfather's querulous voice.

Continually he was finding fault with somebody or something.

For the time being, however, as Gytha rode away on Dragonfly, she forgot everything but the excitement of the Steeple-chase.

She would see once again the man who was inevitably the hero of the stories she told herself at night after she had blown out the candles by her bed.

They rode through the home-park as if going in their usual directions.

It was just in case any of the people in the house might be watching them.

Then doubling back through the woods they set off at a sharp gallop.

They crossed the fields to where about two miles away Lord Locke's boundary adjoined her grandfather's estate.

It was here that there lay the much-contested wood.

It had severed relations between the two families who had lived side by side for so long that it was impossible to think of the County without them.

"Such a stupid feud!" Gytha's mother had once said. "When Papa and I live at the Hall, I have every intention of holding out the hand of friendship to every one of our neighbours, including Lord Locke."

"That is what I shall do if Grandpapa leaves me the house and his money," Gytha told herself.

Then she remembered the conditions which went with it.

For a moment the sunshine was eclipsed and she seemed to be encompassed by a fog that she could not penetrate.

Then she forced herself to forget everything but the excitement of seeing, as she was quite certain she would, Lord Locke win his own Steeple-chase.

They rode slowly through the wood.

When they emerged on the other side of it, Gytha found herself where she wanted to be.

It was on a high rise from which the ground swept down into a valley.

It was there that the Steeple-chase would take place.

She could already see there were a considerable number of spectators standing beside each fence.

As Hawkins had told her, there were now more fences and higher ones than there had ever been in the past.

At the starting-point some of the riders and their horses were already slowly circulating.

All were obviously on very well-bred animals.

Riding them were smart young men who must have come down from London.

There was no mistaking their tall hats set at a jaunty angle on their heads.

Even at a distance Gytha was aware of their meticulously tied cravats, their well-cut riding-jackets and, above all, their highly polished boots.

Then as she was looking from one to another of them, a black stallion came trotting up to the starting-point.

With a leap of her heart she recognised Lord Locke.

There was no one, she thought, who could ride as well as he did.

Nor was there any horse to equal the one he rode.

She looked at him and could see there was little change in his appearance since she had last seen him over a year ago.

If anything, she thought he looked even more handsome than he had then.

Once, out hunting, she had passed him at a gate.

She had been able to look closely at one of the most unusual faces she had ever seen.

It was not only that he was so good-looking.

There was something raffish about him, she thought.

He had the face of a Buccaneer, a Pirate, a man who found life extremely enjoyable and was determined, by hook or by crook, to get the very best of it for himself.

She did not know why she felt she knew so much about a man to whom she had never spoken.

Yet every time she had seen Lord Locke, even in the distance, he seemed to stand out amongst all other men.

Even including the contemporaries by whom he was surrounded.

She could see them now, laughing and talking to him.

Then it was clear he was giving orders, although she could not hear what was said, and they obeyed him.

The horses were now all in line and the spectators were watching them intently.

Until as they moved forward at Lord Locke's command there was the sharp report of the starting-gun, and they were off.

Gytha held her breath.

It was so exciting that, without intending to, she must have urged her horse forward.

He was moving down from the rise and nearer to the race-course.

All the riders had taken the first fence and there was only one refusal at the second.

By the time they got to the third, Gytha could see clearly that Lord Locke's black stallion was ahead.

Not by much, for he was obviously holding him on a tight rein, but definitely ahead.

She was sure that already he was smiling his strange, cynical smile triumphantly.

It was a foregone conclusion that he would win.

On they went, over the water-jump, and now a hedge that seemed even higher than the rest.

There were two falls and another horse ran out.

By now they were reaching the far end of the course.

It was easy to see the fences and that Lord Locke's stallion was taking them effortlessly.

On and on, until finally there was a long stretch down to the winning-post.

It was here, Gytha knew, that Lord Locke was giving his horse its head.

There were only three others left at the front of the field to challenge him.

It was a close finish.

But at the last moment, almost as if Lord Locke lifted his mount to do so, the black stallion spurted forward.

He won what had been a very gruelling Steeple-chase by a length.

Gytha was following it with concentration.

She was willing, although she was not aware of it,

Lord Locke's horse to take every fence.

Down the final stretch to the winning-post she could hardly breathe.

Now that it was over she felt for a moment almost as exhausted as if she had been riding herself.

"What did I tells yer, Miss Gytha?" Hawkins asked. "I knows 'is Lordship'd win. There's nobody as touch 'im—nobody!"

Gytha agreed with him.

But for the moment she could not speak and Hawkins went on:

"It's a pity us can't tell 'im, Miss, how much we've enjoyed watching 'im, an' I'd like ter see that 'orse close to."

"So would I," Gytha replied.

"I've always said," Hawkins continued on conversationally, "'twas a cryin' shame that 'is Lordship's not welcome at t' Hall seein' as how yer father saved his life."

For the first time since the race had begun Gytha turned to look at Hawkins.

Now there was an expression of surprise in her large eyes.

"What do you mean—saved his life?"

"Didn't th' Master ever tell yer about it?" Hawkins enquired.

"No, he did not," Gytha answered. "When did he save Lord Locke's life?"

"'Twas when we were in Portugal, Miss, at th' first battle in which 'is Lordship were engaged after 'e's joined th' Regiment."

"What happened?" Gytha asked.

"We comes upon a troop o' them Frenchies unexpected-like an' afore we knows what's ahappenin', 'is Lordship, tho' he hadn't inherited in them days, had his 'orse shot from under 'im."

Gytha made a little murmur but did not interrupt.

"We were out-numbered by about six ter one," Hawkins continued, "an' yer father had already given orders ter retreat—there were nothin' else we could do—then when Lieutenant Locke crashes to th' ground, 'e pulls in 'is horse, bends down, an' says ter 'im:

"'Jump up behind me, Laddie, an' be darned quick about it!'

"'E gives him a hand, pulls 'im up, then gallops orf wiv bullets whistlin' round 'is ears!"

Gytha gave a sigh.

"It sounds very like Papa!"

"'Twas a miracle, Miss! 'E coulda bin shot down 'imself stayin' behind like that when th' rest o' us, followin' orders, was agalloping off!"

Hawkins laughed and added:

"I bets when 'is Lordship thinks abaht it, he's grateful ter yer father for bein' alive, especially like when 'e wins a race like we've jus' seen."

"I am sure he is," Gytha said quietly.

She looked down below at Lord Locke receiving the congratulations of the crowd clustering around him.

The other riders were coming in slowly.

Then she had an idea!

An idea so fantastic, so revolutionary, that she could hardly dare express it to herself.

chapter two

LORD Locke rode triumphantly with a smile on his rather hard lips towards his house.

There had been the usual congratulations from those who had taken part in the Steeple-chase.

A great number were from the spectators who also wanted to shake his hand.

It was therefore getting on in the afternoon before they finally reached Locke Hall.

Luncheon was awaiting them.

A number of the competitors were by now extremely hungry.

Lord Locke, however, had made it a principle never to ride immediately after a large meal.

He therefore paid no attention to those of his guests who were grumbling at the long delay.

He knew, however, that his Chef would have excelled himself in providing a superlative repast.

He had already before leaving this morning seen his Wine Steward.

He had told him what drinks were to be provided.

He looked forward to Steeple-chases even when he was travelling round the world.

He went to out-of-the-way places, because he had an urge to be, amongst other things, an explorer.

Now he had proved, as he had expected, that his horse was better than anybody else's.

He therefore went out of his way to praise generously the others which he had defeated.

He knew it was to the chagrin of their owners.

However, everybody was very good-humoured about it.

They were, in fact, prepared before the Steeple-chase started for their host to be the winner.

At the front-door of the impressive mansion, which had been rebuilt by his grandfather in the middle of the last century, there was a number of grooms waiting for the riders.

As Lord Locke dismounted, he patted the black stallion who had carried him to victory and said to the groom:

"Hercules behaved exactly as I expected he would, and I know you are as proud of him as I am."

"'E be best 'orse we've 'ad in t' stable, M'Lord," the groom replied.

He knew that Lord Locke agreed with him without his having to say so.

Lord Locke walked up the steps into the Hall with most of his guests following him.

Then he stopped dead.

Standing at the bottom of the stairs, obviously posing deliberately against the gold and crystal balustrade, was a woman.

As Lord Locke stared at her she moved forward.

In a low, sensuous tone he remembered so well, she said:

"Are you pleased to see me, Valiant?"

Surprised was rather the word, Lord Locke thought, or even more appropriately—*astounded*.

24

However, knowing it would be a mistake to say so, he merely replied:

"I was told, Zuleika, that you were out of England."

"I returned to this country two days ago and heard you were here also."

She looked up at him, her eyes saying a great deal more than her lips.

It was impossible to imagine that anybody could be more beautiful.

Princess Zuleika El Saladin was one of those mysterious personalities who suddenly appear like a meteor in the social sky.

They are difficult to fit into any particular category, or, in fact, to understand.

The Princess had appeared in London directly after the war was over.

Her enemies, and of course she had many, said she had been waiting on the "touch-line" to see who was victorious.

Exquisitely beautiful, no one knew exactly what her nationality was or where she came from.

She claimed proudly to be Russian.

Those who grew to know her well, as Lord Locke did, suspected that she more likely came from South of the Black Sea than from North of it.

But she took no one into her confidence.

It was therefore difficult to refute her assertion that she was Russian.

She had been married at one time to a nobleman of her own nationality, and only later to another husband of Turkish origin.

It was his name she used now, calling herself "Princess Zuleika" to which she claimed she was entitled in her own right.

She added "El Saladin" almost as if it were a challenge to those who were obviously curious about her.

Her husbands, if that was the polite name for the men in her life, had between them left her an enormous fortune.

She bought one of the largest houses in Mayfair.

She proceeded to entertain in a manner which was a delight to those who had nothing else to occupy their minds.

Her Balls and Receptions offered all extravegent hospitality and were original in many different ways.

Moreover, they followed each other in quick succession.

Not to be invited was a stigma few people were brave enough to endure.

The Princess had her dark flashing eyes, an exquisitely lissom figure, and jewels which might have come from an Aladdin's cave.

It was obvious she would be pursued by every man in the *Beau Ton*.

But the moment the Princess set eyes on Lord Locke she pursued him relentlessly.

He would have been inhuman if he could have withstood her campaign.

However, he was wise enough to realise he was becoming too deeply involved.

To cut loose from the Princess was one of his reasons for deciding to spend a year travelling around the world.

He visited countries that had been out of reach to Englishmen during the long, isolating years of war.

He had gone to London immediately on his return.

He learnt, and it was a relief, that Princess Zuleika was in France.

Now, when he least expected it, she had reappeared.

Not in London, but in the country, where he had never thought to see her.

He raised her hand to his lips in Continental fashion.

Then he moved across the Hall with her beside him towards the Salon.

He had ordered champagne to be waiting there for him and his guests.

He had chosen his party carefully and had deliberately made it a bachelor gathering.

All of them were competitors in the race, thinking that when men wanted to talk of horses, women were a distraction.

"Do you intend to have luncheon with me?" he asked the Princess as they walked to the Salon.

"Among other things, my dear Valiant," she replied. "In fact, although you omitted to invite me to stay, I am nevertheless here as your guest."

Lord Locke stared at her.

"Have you come alone?" he asked incredulously.

She laughed, and it was a very attractive sound.

"I would not offend your Puritanical sensibilities by doing anything so foolish! No, I have brought with me two chaperones in the shape of Lucy Compton and Caroline Blackstone.

There was a sarcastic twist to Lord Locke's lips as he replied conventionally:

"How delightful!"

He knew that Lady Compton and the Countess Blackstone were each having a wild and indiscreet *affaire de coeur* with riders in his Steeple-chase.

He was quite certain therefore they would have been only too willing to agree to the Princess's suggestion

27

that they should arrive with her at Locke Hall.

Uninvited, but nevertheless to be eagerly accepted by their paramours.

Lord Locke and the Princess had not been in the Salon for more than a few seconds before they were joined by some of the competitors in the Steeple-chase.

A few seconds later Lady Compton and the Countess came in.

There was an expression of surprised delight at their appearance.

Lord Locke thought a little wryly he would now be expected to provide female company for the other men.

They would otherwise feel themselves neglected.

This annoyed him.

He had been much looking forward, after several hectic parties in London, to dinners at which they could talk politics and sport.

Also he wanted to spend the next two days in the saddle.

All that must now be changed with the Princess's arrival.

Short of making a scene, he had no idea how he could get rid of her.

He was well aware that everything that was said or done, if there was anything unusual about it, would be repeated in every Club in St. James's.

He saw that there was a glass of champagne at everybody's side.

He left the room to change his riding-coat and stock before luncheon.

Extremely fastidious, Lord Locke was a follower of the Beau Brummell School.

A gentleman must be spotlessly clean in his habits.

He would not think of sitting down to a meal in a

crumpled shirt or cravat, or in the coat in which he had just been riding.

Despite the time was getting on and he was hungry, he changed his shirt.

Also his coat and cravat, before returning to the Salon.

He felt restored after what had been a really strenuous race.

Nobody seemed to have noticed his absence except the Princess.

She moved at once to his side.

She put her hand, with its long, slender fingers, on his arm.

Looking up into his eyes, she said softly:

"You are pleased to see me again?"

It was difficult for Lord Locke not to give her the answer she required.

Then leaving her, he started to move his guests into the Dining-Room.

As they all expected, the food was outstanding.

The luncheon was a very genial occasion, with everybody toasting him as the winner of his own Steeple-chase.

Also, they were drinking to the beautiful eyes of the three women who had joined them.

Lord Locke, however, realised uncomfortably that the Princess was being indiscreetly familiar.

Despite his long absence abroad, he was again encountering the same difficulties which had sent him from England a year ago.

He was quite certain that the Princess had taken a large number of lovers in his absence.

Yet he had the uncomfortable feeling that in her own way she was true to his memory.

It was not only, as she had told him so often, that he was the most ardent lover she had ever had.

It was also that she had not found anybody of similar social standing to marry her.

It was the knowledge that she was intent on marriage that had frightened Lord Locke away in the first place.

He had told himself so often he had no intention of marrying anyone.

Even if he did, it would certainly not be to a woman who was as outrageously promiscuous as the Princess.

She sharply offended his sensibilities.

At the same time, she was the most passionate and undoubtedly the most beguiling woman he had ever met.

He was well aware before he left England that every one of his contemporaries had been wildly jealous of his position in Princess Zuleika's life.

Lord Locke had enormous self-control.

He had a determination which once he had made up his mind, no one could shake.

He had decided that enough was enough.

He had other things to do in his life besides make love to Zuleika, however attractive she might be.

He knew that everybody was talking about their liaison.

That her brilliant and fantastic parties were given entirely for him.

So he had made his plans and left London unexpectedly.

He let only his most intimate friends know where he was going.

He did not want Zuleika taking it into her head to follow him.

He had bought her a very expensive present. He sent

it to her with a letter thanking her for all she had meant to him.

He made it quite clear that a chapter of their lives was finished.

They would, he said, be unlikely to see each other in the future.

But now, like a Genie in an Eastern story, she was here.

He could not think how he could be rid of her.

He knew how persistent she could be in pursuing anything she wanted.

Even if a man was made of steel or stone, it would be hard to resist her blandishments.

Looking around the Dining-Room table, he was aware that every man present, with the exception of the men beside Lucy Compton and Caroline Blackstone, was fascinated by her as if by a snake.

But once again she was directing her whole being towards him.

He was conscious of her magnetism which had some Oriental power in it that was like magic.

The luncheon had been excellent.

He had been wise enough, knowing they would start late, to order only a few courses.

They therefore rose from the table earlier than might have been expected.

It was, in fact, what ordinarily would have been tea-time when they left the Dining-Room.

"I expect some of you will want to rest after such a strenuous morning, but I am going to the stables to see how our horses are faring."

"I hope they have plenty of champagne to celebrate their achievement in jumping over the new fences!" somebody quipped.

As he walked down the passage, Zuleika put her arm through Lord Locke's to say:

"Do not leave me, Valiant, I want to talk to you."

"I expect we will do that later," he replied. "I have made my plans, Zuleika, not knowing you would surprise me."

Zuleika's lips pouted at him, her eyes narrowed a little.

He knew she was willing him to respond to her as he had done so often in the past.

Almost roughly he shook himself free of her clinging arm.

He left her in the hall and walking out through the front-door, set off towards the stables.

One of his closest friends, Peregrine Westington, caught up with him.

"What are you going to do about the Princess?" he asked bluntly.

Perry had been at School with Lord Locke and had served with him in the same Regiment.

He was one of the few people in whom he ever confided, and he replied now:

"I have no idea! What can I do? I had hoped, Perry, she would have forgotten me."

Peregrine Westington laughed.

"There have been a great many men dancing attendance upon her in your absence, but, to put it bluntly, Valiant, no one you could consider a rival."

Lord Locke's lips tightened and Perry said reflectively:

"It is just like her to spring herself upon you like a leopardess in the jungle."

As he spoke, Lord Locke thought that was exactly what Zuleika was like.

A black leopardess, stalking her prey and springing unawares when least expected.

They had reached the stables by this time, and there was no chance of saying any more.

Lord Locke went from stall to stall, admiring first Hercules, then not only his own horses, but all those which had run in the race.

But part of his mind was busy with the problem of what he could do about Zuleika.

Every instinct warned him not to become involved a second time, as he had been before he went abroad.

Yet, he knew the Princess's persistence.

He could not think how he could circumvent her without causing much uncomfortable and disagreeable gossip.

He was, in fact, at the moment discomfited with a feeling almost of helplessness.

If there was one thing Lord Locke disliked, it was the type of man who left a woman weeping bitterly because she had lost him.

Alternatively she swore vengeance and incited her friends to start up what could become almost a minor war in Social circles.

He had seen it happen so often.

He had always thought the man in question must have played his cards very badly. Or else he was particularly insensitive.

He had enjoyed many love-affairs.

But he had always managed to remain friends with the lady in question when their *affaire de coeur* came to an end.

Although some hearts may have ached, their owners were too proud to humiliate themselves by saying so.

Zuleika was different.

She was in many ways primitive and barbaric, not only in the violence of her love-making, but in her determination to captivate and enslave any man she desired.

Lord Locke knew that if he told Zuleika she could not stay in his house after arriving in such an unprecedented manner, she would undoubtedly contrive to make him appear a brute.

She would arouse half the Social World in her defence.

"What the devil am I to do?" he asked himself.

He reached the last stall and absent-mindedly patted the horse belonging to a friend.

Its groom extolled its good points although Lord Locke did not hear a single word.

He started to walk back towards the house.

Perry was trying to placate him.

"I have been thinking," he said, "that you had better invite some of the neighbours to dine tonight. That at least will relieve the situation a little."

"I have already thought of that," Lord Locke replied. "The difficulty is that when I have been away for so long, they may feel resentful at being invited at the last moment."

"I should tell them the truth," Perry suggested. "Say that some friends have arrived unexpectedly from London and you are therefore turning what was planned as a party for competitors only into something larger."

"I suppose that is what I had better do," Lord Locke said wearily, "but between ourselves, it is a damned nuisance!"

"I agree with you, but it will at least relieve you from having what will in effect be a *tête-à-tête* with Zuleika."

Lord Locke did not reply.

Having entered the house, he went to his Study and wrote half-a-dozen notes.

Then he rang for his Secretary to send grooms posting with the invitations to the nearest houses in the neighbourhood.

"I am hoping these people will be at home, Stevenson," he said to his secretary.

Mr. Stevenson was a middle-aged man who had looked after the house and estate while Lord Locke was away fighting or travelling.

He looked at the names and replied:

"I am sure, My Lord, that all these people are in residence and will be only too delighted to accept Your Lordship's invitation."

"You had better think out a further list of those who might come from farther afield for tomorrow night," Lord Locke said.

"I will do that, My Lord."

"Tonight we will play cards after dinner and for tomorrow you had better engage a Band of some sort."

Mr. Stevenson did not show, even by the flicker of an eye-lid, that he was surprised.

He was used to His Lordship changing his plans.

He did not appear to think it impossible at a moment's notice in the depth of the country to find an orchestra.

He was aware it would be expected to be of outstanding excellence.

He merely bowed, and, taking the letters, left the room.

He carried out his instructions so efficiently that ten minutes later the grooms were leaving the stables on fast horses.

Lord Locke, to give himself and the household time,

had ordered dinner unfashionably late.

He knew that would be a surprise in itself.

He thought however that, if they were available, most of his neighbours would be consumed with curiosity to see him now he had returned.

Also they would wish to find out who had joined what was reputed to be a bachelor party.

He was thinking that he must tell his other guests what had been planned.

The door of his Study opened and Zuleika came in.

She looked so lovely that it was impossible for Lord Locke not to admire the brilliance of her dark eyes in the perfect oval of her face.

Her hair was jet black with mauve lights in it.

It made a striking contrast to her magnolia skin, which any man who saw it longed to touch.

Her gowns were always moulded to display every curve of her perfect figure.

As she moved sinuously towards Lord Locke, he thought a little cynically that she appeared to be naked beneath her gown.

It was more than likely that was the truth.

She did not speak, but simply walked across the room until she stood in front of him.

Then without touching him she tried to put pressure on him by the power of thought and the magnetism of her desire.

For a moment they just looked into each other's eyes.

Until with what was obviously an effort Lord Locke walked away to stand with his back to the fireplace.

"You should not have come here, Zuleika. It will cause a great deal of unnecessary and unpleasant gossip."

"Why should we care?" Zuleika asked.

Her low voice was somehow as sensual as if she actually declared her passionate desire for him.

"I have to think of my family," Lord Locke answered loftily. "Before I left England, my grandmother was complaining that we were being talked about, and I do not want that to happen again."

Zuleika laughed, and it was derisively.

"Dearest, foolish Valiant, do you really think I care what your grandmother or anyone else says? I have missed you, I want you, and now that you are back we can be together as I always intended us to be."

There was a determination in the last few words that made Lord Locke angry.

"I think, Zuleika," he replied, "I should make myself very clear. I admire you, I want us always to be friends, but in my position it would be a mistake for people to know too much about my private life."

He paused to smile beguilingly before he added:

"And as you are well aware, it is very difficult to be private where you are concerned."

"It is something I have no intention of attempting," Zuleika retorted. "You know what I want, Valiant, or do I have to tell you?"

She spoke in a low voice.

Walking very slowly, she reached his side again.

Then she threw back her head.

She looked so beautiful that it seemed impossible for any man to refuse her.

The invitation in her eyes and the provocation of her lips were irresistible.

Lord Locke did not move.

After a second she said so softly that he could hardly hear the words:

"Must I ask you what you will not ask me?"

It was then, when he was wondering frantically what he should say, the door opened.

To his utter relief Perry walked in.

He saw at a glance what was happening.

In an ordinary, conversational tone he said:

"Oh, here you are, Valiant! I thought I should warn you that somebody has called to see you and insists on speaking to you however busy you may be!"

"That sounds as if somebody has come to complain," Lord Locke managed to reply.

He turned away from the Princess, saying as he did so:

"I am sorry, Zuleika, but I suggest you rest before dinner, which will be late because we are being joined by a number of my neighbours as guests."

Just for a moment there was a flash of anger in her eyes.

She realised immediately why they had been invited.

Then in dulcet tones, almost like the cooing of a dove, she said:

"A party! How delightful, and how sweet of you, dearest Valiant, to give it in my honour!"

She reached out to touch his arm as she passed him and to smile up into his face.

Then she glided from the room so gracefully that her feet hardly seemed to touch the floor.

Only as the door shut behind her did Lord Locke give a sigh of relief and say:

"Thank God, Perry, that you came in when you did!"

"I thought perhaps you might be in trouble, old boy, when I saw Zuleika was not with the others in the Salon."

He paused before he asked a little tentatively, because he knew his friend's dislike of any interference in his private affairs:

"Was she actually proposing to you?"

Lord Locke nodded, then he said angrily:

"How the hell have I managed to get myself into such a position? I can hardly spend the rest of my life going round the world to avoid her."

"No, of course not," Perry said sympathetically. "All the same, it would be a mistake to have a scene with all our friends here. You know how Charlie for one would chatter, and Tony for another."

Lord Locke groaned.

Before he could speak, however, the door opened and the Butler said:

"Miss Sullivan asks, M'Lord, if you could see her as soon as possible, as she is eager to return home."

"So there really was someone wishing to see me!" Lord Locke asked his friend.

"I told you so," Perry replied, "and actually it was as good an excuse as any other."

Then Lord Locke said reflectively to the Butler:

"Surely, Bates, you do not mean a relative of Sir Robert?"

"His granddaughter, M'Lord."

"Here? Calling on me?" Lord Locke ejaculated. "Wonders will never cease! Show her in, Bates. I am full of curiosity as to why Miss Sullivan should be here."

There was a faint smile on the old Butler's lips.

He was well aware of the feud which had existed between the two big land-owners ever since he had been in service. When he went from the Study, Lord Locke said:

"I had always understood ever since I was a child that the name of Sullivan must never pass my lips, and their footsteps should never encroach upon our land."

"If she is going to complain about the much-contested wood, I am going to leave you," Perry said. "I can remember when I was a Schoolboy your father ranting about it."

He laughed before he said:

"I thought then that any man with an atom of sense could have divided it down the middle and accepted that as the reasonable solution."

Lord Locke laughed.

"I am sure nothing so simple would ever have occurred to my father. He was determined to win the contest, and so was 'Old Groaner,' as we used to call Sir Robert!"

Perry laughed, then he walked to the door.

"I wish you luck with the 'Old Groaner's' granddaughter, but be careful! She might prove to be as dangerous as Zuleika!"

He did not wait for a reply but walked away.

Two minutes later the door opened and Bates announced:

"Miss Gytha Sullivan, M'Lord!"

Lord Locke had somehow expected that Sir Robert's granddaughter would be a hearty, horsy woman of uncertain age.

To his surprise the young girl who came into the room was small and slight.

She was wearing a dark riding-habit which threw into prominence, under her riding-hat, the gold of her hair.

She had a small heart-shaped face with huge grey eyes.

Surprisingly they were encircled by much darker

lashes which turned up like a child's.

It gave her a very young and appealing expression.

As she moved towards Lord Locke he thought that her eyes held in their depths an expression of shyness.

Then it struck him that it might be one of fear.

He held out his hand, saying:

"This is a great surprise, Miss Sullivan, and I must of course, welcome you for the first time to Locke Hall."

"It is just as . . . magnificent as I thought it would . . . be," Gytha said in a soft little voice. "Thank you . . . for seeing . . . me."

"I am delighted," Lord Locke said, "if it means that ridiculous feud which has raged between our two families for over thirty years has come to an end."

"I am afraid I cannot speak on behalf of my grandfather, who does not know I am here," Gytha replied, "but where I am concerned . . . I have always . . . wanted to meet . . . you."

Lord Locke smiled, and she added:

"But first I must congratulate you on winning a magnificent Steeple-chase."

He raised his eye-brows.

"Are you telling me you saw it?"

She nodded, and there was a hint of mischief in her eyes as she said:

"I watched it, as I have watched your Steeple-chases in the past, from the Rise."

Lord Locke knew this was just in front of the much-contested wood and he therefore laughed.

"So you were asserting your rights to it!" he said with mock severity.

"The only thing in which I was interested," Gytha replied, "was in watching your horse . . . who was utterly and completely . . . magnificent!"

She wanted to add that so was his rider.

She was aware, now that she was actually talking to Lord Locke, that he was more attractive than she had thought he would be.

She had never seen him without a hat.

She liked the way his hair grew back from his square forehead, while his eye-brows were strongly marked over his eyes.

He certainly looked like a Buccaneer or a Pirate.

At the same time, no one could take him for anything but an aristocrat.

"Will you sit down?" he suggested.

Gytha seated herself on a sofa at the side of the fire-place, and there was silence.

She looked up and felt her heart beating frantically in her breast.

She wondered if she dare tell him what was in her mind.

Then, as if Lord Locke were perceptively aware of her difficulty, he said:

"I am waiting with the greatest curiosity to know why you have come to see me, but first let me offer you some refreshment: a glass of champagne, perhaps?"

Gytha shook her head.

"No . . . no! I want nothing . . . except to . . . tell you . . . why I have . . . come."

She looked away from him as she spoke.

He was aware now that she was very shy.

She had taken off her gloves as she sat down.

Then she began twisting her fingers together.

"I cannot imagine what is worrying you," Lord Locke said quietly, "unless of course it is once again the question of the wood."

"It is not that," Gytha replied. "It is something which

concerns . . . myself alone . . . in fact, I have . . . come to ask Your Lordship for . . . your help."

"Of course I am only too willing to give it, if it is possible."

"I am afraid when you hear what I am asking . . . you will . . . think it very . . . very strange."

"Shall I say I am willing to listen and to try to understand what it is that you require of me."

Because he thought he might seem less intimidating, Lord Locke seated himself in an armchair close to the sofa.

Then as he realised how shy Gytha was he said:

"I am really eager to help you."

He spoke in a voice that few women could resist.

Gytha gave him a tremulous smile before she said:

"I learnt only today from my father's batman that Papa . . . saved your life when you . . . first entered the Regiment."

"Of course he did," Lord Locke agreed, "and I have always been very grateful to him."

He paused before he went on:

"And may I tell you what a magnificent Commander your father was. I was very proud, as we all were, to serve under him."

He saw that Gytha was listening intently and he continued:

"I was not with him when he was killed at Waterloo, as I had been posted to another Battalion. Although I could not write to tell your family so, I was extremely sorry to hear, after the battle was over, that he had not survived."

"It was when Papa went to the war that my mother and I went to . . . live with my . . . grandfather in the Big House."

Lord Locke did not speak, and she went on:

"Mama died . . . and as Grandpapa is very old . . . I have been alone with him this . . . past year and seen nobody except occasionally when I have been out . . . hunting."

She wanted Lord Locke to know how very restricted her life had been.

She thought he understood before she went on:

"A few weeks ago the doctors told . . . me that my grandfather . . . cannot . . . live for more than two or at the outside three . . . months."

"I am sorry to hear that," Lord Locke replied conventionally.

"I think in a way," Gytha said, "it will be a relief for him, because he is often in pain and it makes him . . . very disagreeable. But he is . . . as I expect you know . . . a very . . . rich man."

"That is what I have always heard," Lord Locke replied.

He was wondering what this had to do with him.

"Grandpapa has . . . decided," Gytha continued, "that I am to be his . . . heir."

She said the words in a dull voice that was almost one of despair.

Lord Locke looked puzzled before he murmured:

"I must of course congratulate you."

"It is not . . . something I . . . want," Gytha retorted. "In fact, I would much rather Grandpapa had left me . . . just enough to live on . . . but unfortunately he has made up his . . . mind and . . . nothing I can say has . . . any effect."

Lord Locke was wondering what he should say to this.

Gytha, twisting her fingers together once again, said:

"I have always been told that you have . . . sworn you will . . . never marry."

"That is true," Lord Locke said. "I have no intention of marrying and, as I am not yet thirty, it will be many years before it is necessary for me to have an heir."

He smiled at her before he added:

"At the same time, I can see it could be very difficult for you to decide to take up the same attitude, if that is what you want."

He could not imagine where this conversation was leading.

But because Gytha was so distressed and, he thought, rather pathetic, he was trying to do his best.

"Grandpapa has insisted," Gytha explained haltingly, "that I must marry one of his nephews, either Vincent or Jonathan Sullivan and I . . . detest them . . . both."

She made a sound which was almost a sob.

"Whatever I say . . . because I am only eighteen . . . and Grandpapa is my Guardian . . . I shall be . . . forced to do so. There is no way by which I can . . . prevent it . . . unless you will . . . help me."

She did not wait for Lord Locke to say anything but went on:

"I . . . I thought . . . if you were really grateful to my father for . . . saving your life . . . you might feel it was a . . . debt of honour . . . and you would . . . therefore not refuse to do what I am . . . asking."

"What are you asking?" Lord Locke enquired.

Gytha took a deep breath.

"That . . . that you will . . . become . . . engaged to me."

chapter three

LORD Locke stiffened and as he stared at Gytha in sheer astonishment she said quickly:

"It would be an . . . engagement only until Grand-papa . . . dies . . . then of course . . . it will be . . . can-celled."

"I do not understand."

"If I am . . . engaged to . . . you," Gytha replied, "then I cannot be . . . forced into . . . marriage with . . . one of my cousins."

"Are you sure that your grandfather will insist on a marriage for which you have no inclination?"

"I have already tried to . . . persuade him that it is something I . . . cannot do . . . and he merely . . . flew into a rage and told me, as my Guardian, I had to . . . obey him."

Gytha drew a deep breath, then said hesitatingly:

"I believe that is the . . . law, and because they want Grandpapa's . . . money, my cousins will be only . . . too willing to . . . marry me."

Lord Locke did not speak, and after a moment she went on in a frightened voice:

"In the past Vincent always . . . appeared to . . . dislike me and treated me with . . . contempt . . . and Jonathan is even more . . . unpleasant, and he has . . . wet . . . flabby . . . hands."

She shivered as she spoke.

Lord Locke knew she was thinking she could not bear such a man to touch her.

What she was asking was, of course, impossible!

He rose to his feet and walked across the room.

He stood at the window, looking out onto the sunlit garden.

He was wondering how he could explain to this impulsive girl that what she was asking was really quite ridiculous.

Then as he stood there staring out at the trees turning to autumn hues he heard a sound.

Turning round, he saw that Gytha had reached the door.

"Where are you going?" he asked sharply.

She stood still as he spoke.

There was something about her which reminded him of a School-girl who had been caught out doing something wrong.

"It was a . . . mistake to . . . come here," she said after a moment. "But I was so . . . desperate and when I . . . learnt that my father had . . . saved your life I thought perhaps . . . you would . . . understand."

Her words seemed to fall over each other and Lord Locke said:

"Come and sit down again, and let us see if we can find a solution to your problem."

He paused a moment before continuing:

"I would not want you to think I am ungrateful for having been able to live for very much longer than the French intended."

He smiled at her as he spoke in a way which most women found irresistible.

Gytha did not move.

"I think . . . perhaps I should go . . . home."

Lord Locke was trying to think of some way of assisting her.

It was then he realised that this could be his answer to Princess Zuleika.

He was so astonished at what Gytha had asked of him, so bewildered by her problem.

He had for a moment forgotten his own problems.

Now it was almost as if he could see the pieces of a jig-saw puzzle falling into place.

He realised this would make it impossible for Zuleika to behave in such an outrageous manner.

In two months she might easily have transferred her affections elsewhere.

"Come and sit down," he said.

There was an authoritative note in his voice which made Gytha obey him.

But he was also aware that she moved warily.

She was almost like a small animal who was afraid of being trapped.

Once again she sat down on the edge of the sofa.

She raised her worried eyes to his.

Lord Locke thought she was in fact one of the prettiest young women he had seen for a long time.

He did not sit down.

Once again he stood with his back to the fireplace as he said:

"Now let us talk this out together sensibly. Your grandfather is determined to make you his heir, but he insists that you marry one of your cousins because he is afraid of fortune-hunters."

He paused, and after a moment Gytha said hesitatingly:

"That is what . . . frightens him . . . but he . . . could not think . . . that is what . . . you are."

49

"That is true," Lord Locke agreed, "but because my family has been at daggers drawn with yours for so many years, he may well refuse to countenance such a marriage."

"I thought of . . . that when I was coming . . . here," Gytha said, "but I have a . . . feeling although I may be wrong . . . that Grandpapa was . . . interested in the stories he heard of your . . . bravery and of the . . . medals you have won for . . . gallantry."

Her voice was very moving as she added:

"He was so . . . proud of Papa and I have always . . . thought that he . . . despised Vincent and Jonathan for not . . . fighting in . . . the war."

"I see your reasoning," Lord Locke said, "but I can hardly expect him to welcome me with open arms. Perhaps, however, he might consent to a secret engagement if nothing else, which would at least give us time."

Almost as if he had asked the question, Gytha said:

"The doctors were very . . . insistent that Grandpapa cannot . . . live for very much . . . more than . . . two months, if as . . . long as . . . that."

There was silence, then she added:

"But I know now it was most impertinent of me to come . . . to you."

"I think actually it was very sensible," Lord Locke answered, "and I certainly owe your father a debt which can never be repaid in full."

"Perhaps it was . . . wrong of . . . me to . . . remind you of . . . it."

"No, it was right, absolutely right," Lord Locke said firmly, "and that is why . . . Miss Sullivan, I am prepared to do as you ask me, on condition, of course, that our engagement ends after your grandfather is no longer with us."

Gytha clasped her hands together as she whispered:

"Do you . . . mean it? Do you . . . really mean . . . it?"

"I mean it," Lord Locke said, "and I think you have handled the situation so intelligently that you must suggest to me exactly how I should approach your grandfather."

"First I want to . . . thank you," Gytha said. "I was thinking . . . that if you . . . refused, as in fact I expected you would, I would have to . . . kill myself rather than marry . . . anyone as . . . horrible as either of my . . . cousins."

"You must not talk like that," Lord Locke exclaimed. "You are young, you are lovely, and you have, I am sure, a delightful and very interesting life ahead of you."

He smiled before he added:

"This is only the first fence, and there will doubtless be a great number of others."

Gytha gave him a shy little smile before she said:

"If I can take the fences as your horse took those in your Steeple-chase this afternoon . . . I shall have no more . . . worries."

"I can only hope that is true," Lord Locke replied, "and now Miss Sullivan—or perhaps I should call you by your Christian name as we are supposed to be engaged—what do you want me to do?"

"I thought . . . as my cousins are . . . arriving tomorrow," Gytha replied, "it is . . . important for you to meet Grandpapa . . . this evening rather than early tomorrow morning, when usually he is not at his . . . best."

"I understand," Lord Locke agreed. "So I will come back with you now."

Gytha drew in her breath.

He knew by the expression in her eyes that was what she wanted.

Then as he looked at the clock he had an idea.

"I will come to speak to your grandfather," he said, "and at the same time, because it will help me, I should be extremely grateful if you would dine here with me tonight."

"Dine with . . . you?"

He saw she had never thought of such an idea.

"It is obvious that that is what we would both want," he said, "if we were really engaged to be married."

"Yes . . . of course . . . but if you have a party . . . they might think it rather . . . strange."

"What I am going to suggest to you," Lord Locke said, working it out in his own mind, "is that we keep our engagement secret except from just two or three very close friends."

Gytha nodded agreement and he went on:

"But the announcement will seem—much more credible if we are seen together previously in each other's company rather than if you are suddenly produced as some mythical figure they have never heard of before."

"Yes . . . of course I see . . . what you . . . mean," Gytha murmured nervously.

As she spoke she realised that never for one moment had she visualised being involved in Lord Locke's life.

She was hoping that he should appear in hers, like Perseus rescuing Andromeda.

She was, however, intelligent enough to understand what he was suggesting, and after a moment she said:

"If that is what you want . . . I will come to . . . dinner but I hope . . . because I am very unused to parties and to meeting . . . strangers I shall not . . . disgrace you."

"I am sure that is impossible," Lord Locke said, "and now, as time is getting on, how do you suggest I travel with you to see your grandfather?"

"I . . . I rode here."

"That makes things very much easier and certainly far quicker if we ride across country," Lord Locke said.

He pulled the bell beside the fireplace as he spoke.

When Bates opened the door he said:

"I am going home with Miss Sullivan, and I want a horse immediately. Also, Bates, tell Mr. Stevenson that Miss Sullivan will be my guest at dinner."

"Very good, M'Lord."

Bates was too well trained to show his surprise.

But he could not completely suppress a hint of curiosity in his old eyes.

As he shut the door Lord Locke said:

"Now I insist, Gytha, on your having a glass of champagne, not only because I think you will need it, but also because we should drink a toast to the success of our little scheme."

He walked across to the grog-tray as he spoke.

He poured out two glasses of champagne from the open bottle that was resting in a silver ice-bucket.

He carried the glasses towards her.

Gytha rose to her feet, and he thought how small and fragile she looked.

Also very much in need of protection.

She took a glass from him.

Before he could speak she raised it, saying:

"To Hercules . . . and his very . . . kind owner!"

Lord Locke laughed.

"You have beaten me to the post, Gytha, for of course I had intended to toast you. Nevertheless let me say I hope we will both be as successful as Hercules, and I think you were very brave to come to me for help."

"I was very . . . frightened," Gytha admitted, "and I still . . . am."

"I think really it is I who should be afraid," Lord Locke said. "I have always believed your grandfather to be a very ferocious and formidable enemy."

Gytha felt this was a rather good description of her grandfather.

At the same time, as she did not wish to anticipate the worst, she said:

"He is very old and extremely ill, although he will not acknowledge it."

She drank only a little of the champagne.

Then Bates announced that the horse was being brought round from the stables.

"I think we should leave now," Lord Locke said.

Gytha preceded him out of the Study.

As she reached the Hall she saw a tall, good-looking young man was standing there.

"I hear you are going out, Valiant," he said to Lord Locke.

As he spoke his eyes were on Gytha.

"I have something important to see to, Perry," Lord Locke replied. "If I am late, please look after my guests until I return."

Peregrine's eyebrows were raised.

"Miss Sullivan is dining with us," Lord Locke went on.

He added to Gytha who had moved a little way from them:

"May I introduce my great friend, Peregrine Westington, who also served under your father in Portugal."

There was no doubting the sudden light that came into Gytha's eyes at the mention of her father's name.

She held out her hand.

"Perhaps one day we could talk about him?" she said.

"That would give me great pleasure," Perry replied.

Lord Locke could see the horses waiting for them at the bottom of the steps.

He hurried Gytha away towards them.

He was aware as he did so that Perry was looking at him with a puzzled expression in his eyes.

Gytha knew they had very little time.

She therefore set the pace as they rode across the fields. She took a direct route.

It made the distance between the two big houses far less than if they had kept to the road.

Dragonfly acquitted himself well.

But Gytha could not pretend that he was not out-classed by Lord Locke's horse.

He was nearly as magnificent as the black stallion on which he had won his Steeple-chase.

Only as they drew near to her home did Gytha begin to feel very nervous.

She had not reasoned out to herself what she would do if her grandfather threw himself into one of his rages.

If he insisted on Lord Locke leaving the house.

Remembering what had happened in the past, she could not even be sure that he would not call for the servants to have him flung out.

Then her perception she had never known to be wrong told her that in his heart he despised both his nephews.

He disliked the idea of their being able to spend his money.

As they reached the front-door, a groom came hurrying from the stables to take their horses.

She saw the astonishment in his face at seeing Lord Locke beside her.

It made her remember for how many years the feud between the two families had existed.

There had been no communication of any sort between them except for letters of abuse.

They walked side by side up the steps.

With a hint of amusement in his voice Lord Locke said:

"Do not be frightened. This is our 'Waterloo,' and we have to be victorious."

She flashed him a little smile of gratitude.

There was, however, a distinct tremor in her voice as she asked one of the footmen:

"Where . . . is . . . Sir Robert?"

"In the Library, Miss," he replied. "He were askin' for yer a short time ago."

Gytha walked towards the Library with Lord Locke beside her.

As she went she pulled off her riding-hat.

He thought her fair hair was like a ray of sunshine in the darkness of the corridor.

A footman opened the door of the Library.

As Gytha walked in followed by Lord Locke she saw her grandfather in his wheelchair.

He was sitting in the window, looking out at the setting sun.

There was, however, a scowl between his eyes.

She knew without being told that he was angry because she had not been available when he wanted her.

She was, however, relieved to see that Dobson, his valet, was not with him.

She walked across the room.

Sir Robert turned his head to say in a disagreeable voice:

"So here you are, and about time too!"

It was then he saw Lord Locke behind her.

He stared at him with an undisguised curiosity.

Gytha went to her grandfather's side.

In a very small, frightened voice she said:

"I have brought . . . Lord Locke to meet you . . . Grandpapa and to . . . tell you that we are . . . engaged to be . . . married."

"Locke? Did you say Locke?" the old man roared.

Lord Locke held out his hand.

"I am delighted to meet you, Sir Robert. It is something I have been wanting to do for years. I am sure you will agree that it is time we ceased to allow anything so unimportant as Monk's Wood to divide our two families."

Sir Robert stared at him.

"Are you telling me that you are the young man who now owns the Hall in which I have not set foot for over twenty-five years?"

"I am, Sir Robert, and now that my father is dead and I wish to become engaged to your granddaughter, I would like to give you a peace-offering in the shape of Monk's Wood."

"A peace-offering? What the devil do you mean by that?" Sir Robert demanded. "Monk's Wood belongs to me, and always has!"

"Then shall I say that I will not only relinquish all claims to it, but will also ensure that it no longer figures on the maps of the Locke estate."

"I should hope not," Sir Robert snapped. "It was disgraceful putting it there in the first place!"

"I am quite prepared to agree with you on that," Lord Locke replied benignly.

"You are, are you? 'Soft-soaping' me, I suppose, because you have your eye on my granddaughter!"

"You can hardly blame me for that, Sir," Lord Locke replied. "She is an unusually lovely girl!"

"You doubtless also have your eyes on the fortune she will inherit when I die," Sir Robert said sourly.

"On the contrary, Sir," Lord Locke replied. "My father left me very comfortably 'warm in the pocket,' and I have no interest whatever in any dowry my future wife might bring with her."

"'Warm in the pocket,' eh?" Sir Robert said with interest. "I have often wondered if he was as rich as he professed to be."

"I can assure you, any stories you have heard about his wealth were not exaggerated."

There was a little silence.

Gytha was afraid her grandfather might be insulting to Lord Locke.

She put her hand on his arm and said:

"Please, Grandpapa, allow me to become engaged to Lord Locke."

"I was just wondering," Sir Robert answered shrewdly, "how you have had the audacity to be acquainted with this man when it has been forbidden to mention his name in this house."

"Be honest, Grandpapa," Gytha said softly. "I would not mind betting that you know already how brilliantly Lord Locke won the Steeple-chase that took place on his land this morning."

"A close finish, from all I hear," Sir Robert growled.

Gytha gave a cry of delight.

"Then you did know! I was quite certain you could not resist being interested. I only wish you could have seen the race. It was absolutely thrilling! And the jumps were higher than they have ever been before!"

Her grandfather gave her a sharp glance.

What she said confirmed his suspicions that she had attended other Steeple-chases that had taken place on the forbidden territory.

Then, as if he were prepared to play his part as things seemed to be going so well, Lord Locke said:

"What I would like to do, Sir Robert, if it interests you, is to ride my stallion who won the race over here one day soon so that you can see him. I believe him to be a very exceptional horse, and I would value your opinion on him."

"You would, would you?" Sir Robert said. "Well, I suppose, as I cannot move out of this damned chair, you had better bring the animal to me, and the sooner the better, from all I know about my health."

It was so like him, Gytha thought, to be aware that his days were numbered.

No one had dared tell him so.

Because he was being so amenable, she said:

"Now that you have seen Lord Locke, Grandpapa, and know what a magnificent rider he is, you will understand why I want to marry him."

Sir Robert looked at her from under belittling eyebrows.

"You prefer him, I suppose, to one of your cousins?"

"He served under Papa," Gytha said, "and although I did not know it until quite recently . . . Papa once saved his . . . life."

"I was aware of that."

"You were? You never told me!"

"I told your father it was a great mistake to fraternise with the enemy."

Sir Robert spoke harshly.

At the same time there was an undoubted twinkle in his eye and Lord Locke laughed.

"Personally, Sir, I am very grateful to be alive, and I think now perhaps it was fate that brought Gytha and me together."

"If you ask me, it was gross deception, sneaking about behind my back," Sir Robert growled.

"You must please forgive me, Grandpapa," Gytha said.

"I do not know about that," Sir Robert replied. "One should not rush into these things. It does not necessarily follow that because a man is a good horseman he will also make a good husband!"

There was a short silence before Gytha faltered:

"If you will allow us to be . . . secretly engaged while you get to know Lord Locke and will, I am certain, come to approve of him, then you can tell Vincent and Jonathan there is no point in . . . either of them . . . offering for . . . me."

Gytha's voice trembled on the last words.

It told Lord Locke, as he listened to her, how frightened she was.

He was therefore not surprised when Sir Robert said:

"So that is how the wind blows! To avoid marriage with your cousins you are prepared to accept the attentions of any hobbledehoy you happen to meet!"

"Oh, Grandpapa, that is not fair!" Gytha said. "You can hardly call Lord Locke with all his decorations a hobbledehoy!"

The old man did not reply.

Gytha had the idea he was, in fact, a little ashamed of what he had said.

Then as if he must assert himself he growled:

"Have it your own way, but I will have nothing made public, you understand, until I know Locke better than I do at the moment and am convinced he is not bribing me with a wood I already own."

"I would like you to consider, Sir," Lord Locke said, "that if and when Gytha and I are married, the two estates will be merged, making a whole which will be the most important in the County and will certainly exceed that of any other land owner."

Gytha knew this was a telling argument.

It was one which her grandfather would appreciate.

But as if he did not wish to appear to agree too readily to what had been suggested, he said:

"A secret engagement, and not a word to anyone, do you understand? Not a word! I will have no puffing and blowing in *The Gazette* until I know a great deal more about you, young man, and it had better be to your advantage."

Then before Lord Locke could speak he shouted:

"I am tired! It is time I went to bed. Where is Dobson?"

Even as he said the words the door opened.

Gytha knew that as usual her grandfather's valet had been listening at the door.

He hurried to the back of the wheelchair, saying as he did so:

"I'm here, Sir Robert, an' it's after your bedtime."

"I know that, you fool!" Sir Robert replied. "It is what I have just said! Take me upstairs."

Gytha bent forward and kissed his cheek.

"Goodnight, Grandpapa, and thank you for being so kind. Lord Locke and I will do exactly as you have suggested."

"You had better make sure of that," the old man retorted, "or I will have no more billing and cooing between you! Then you will marry a man whom I choose."

With that parting shot Dobson pushed the wheelchair out of the room.

They could still hear Sir Robert's voice growling at his valet as he was taken down the passage.

Gytha felt her legs would no longer support her.

She sank down into an armchair.

"I am . . . sorry," she said a little faintly.

"Is he always so querulous?" Lord Locke asked sympathetically.

"Querulous!" Gytha repeated. "I assure you, he was charming, delightful, and in every way very different from what he usually is."

She sighed.

"He rants, roars, and takes everybody to task, usually for something they have not done."

"And you have put up with this for a long time?"

"Ever since Mama . . . died. And being alone with him in this big house is very . . . very . . . difficult."

"I can understand that," Lord Locke said, "but at least you will have a change of scene this evening."

He moved towards the door, saying:

"Go up and dress, Gytha, so that you will look your best for the party tonight, and I will send a carriage for you in an hour's time."

"I could use . . . Grandpapa's carriage," Gytha suggested tentatively.

"I am quite sure it would annoy your grandfather to have his horses taken out at night," Lord Locke replied, "while mine could do with some exercise! Do not be late, for there is somebody I want you to meet before dinner."

He did not explain who this was.

Before Gytha could ask any questions, she could already hear his footsteps going down the passage.

'I never thanked him,' she thought.

Then she remembered it would be something she could do that evening.

Only when she ran upstairs to change did she wish she had not agreed to dine at Locke Hall.

She was sure that there would be a very large party.

It would be difficult to explain her presence.

She supposed that other people who lived in the neighbourhood would also be guests.

They would certainly think it very strange to find her in Lord Locke's company.

It was all very complicated.

But she could hardly believe that her plan had been so successful.

Her grandfather had agreed not to force her immediately into marriage with one of her cousins.

Lord Locke might think her grandfather was being difficult. She knew, as she had told him, that she had never known him so amenable.

In his own way he had been content with what had been arranged.

'He is really quite pleased,' she thought, 'that I am to marry Lord Locke and that the two estates are to be joined.'

It seems wrong to deceive what was a dying man.

She persuaded herself, however, that it was excusable.

Nothing could be more ghastly than to be married to either Vincent or Jonathan.

"If you're agoin' to dinner, Miss, what gown are you agoin' to wear?" the housemaid who always looked after her asked.

It was then that Gytha was awake to a cold reality.

She would be attending a very fashionable dinner-party with Lord Locke's friends, and she had nothing suitable to wear.

There had never been any point in buying any elegant gowns.

Even if she could have persuaded her grandfather to provide them for her, there had seemed no need.

There had been nowhere for her to go.

She ate her dinner alone on a tray in the sitting-room which opened out of her bedroom.

Occasionally when her cousins or other relations were in the house, they ate in the big Dining-Room.

"How can I go to Locke Hall in anything I have at the moment?" Gytha asked herself in a panic.

How could she appear like Cinderella or worse, the goose-girl at the feast?

Yet Lord Locke said he would tell just the few intimate friends that they were engaged to be married.

She knew she must not let him down.

He had been so kind and so understanding!

Finally she let Emily help her into a simple gown of sprigged muslin.

The seamstress who came to the house to repair the linen had made it for her.

The muslin was from a roll of material her mother had bought several years before she died.

The seamstress had copied it painstakingly from a

gown illustration in *The Ladies Journal*.

The caption said it was worn by one of the most beautiful hostesses in London.

Gytha feared it was very inadequate.

Yet it was certainly better than anything else she possessed.

Actually, because she was so slim, it made her look very young.

At the same time, insubstantial, as if she were not human but a nymph from the woods.

There were ribbons the very pale green of young leaves which crossed over her breast and cascaded down her back.

The gown was trimmed at the hem and around the small puffed sleeves with little frills of its own material.

Then it was edged with narrow shadow lace that might have been made by fairy fingers.

The only jewellery which Gytha possessed was a necklace of small pearls.

Her father had given it to her mother on the first anniversary of their wedding.

He had never had much money to spend.

Sir Robert believed that anything in the way of presents should be made only by him, and not by anybody else.

The pearl necklace had therefore been her mother's most prized possession.

As she put it on, Gytha prayed that her mother would guide and help her.

She was sure that her father had protected her and saved her from having to marry one of her cousins.

She said a little prayer to both of them.

"Thank you, Papa, for saving Lord Locke's life so

that he felt under an obligation to help me, and help me, Mama, so that he will not feel ashamed of me tonight."

When the carriage arrived, it was larger and more luxurious than she had expected.

It was drawn by far better horses than anything in her grandfather's stables.

The footman covered her knees with a fur rug as she drove away.

Gytha wished she did not feel so shy and so frightened.

This was, in fact, an adventure that she thought one day, if she ever did marry, she could tell her children.

It was, of course, wildly exciting to be going back to Locke Hall.

She had been inside it today for the first time in her life.

She would be able to talk to and look at Lord Locke himself.

Never had she dreamt when she had watched him win a Steeple-chase or saw him out hunting that she would ever have the chance to talk to him.

Let alone, through an outrageous suggestion of her own, had she dreamt she would pretend to be engaged to him.

"I am grateful . . . so very . . . grateful!" she whispered.

The carriage turned into the courtyard outside the Hall.

She could see the red carpet laid down over the grey stone steps.

The light was shining through the open front-door.

The footmen in their elaborate livery were waiting.

She felt her heart beating tumultuously.

Her shyness made her want to run away and hide.

Then a pride that she had not realised she possessed came to her rescue.

As she stepped from the carriage she walked slowly and with what she hoped was dignity up the red carpeted steps.

She reached the brilliantly lit Hall.

"Good-evening, Miss," Bates said respectfully. "It's a great pleasure to welcome you back here again."

Gytha gave him a little smile.

He escorted her across the Hall past a door which she supposed would lead into the Grand Salon.

Turning right, he led her down a passage.

As Bates stopped she remembered this was where she had been that afternoon.

It was, in fact, Lord Locke's Study.

"Miss Gytha Sullivan!" Bates announced.

As she entered, Gytha saw there were two men in the room.

One of them was Lord Locke, resplendent in his evening-clothes with knee-breeches and silk stockings.

The other was the young man she had met that afternoon and who was called Perry.

Lord Locke walked towards her.

When he reached her, to her surprise he took her hand in his.

He raised it Continental fashion perfunctorily to his lips.

"You are very punctual," he said, "and I am indeed grateful."

"I hear, Miss Sullivan," Perry interspersed, "that I have to congratulate my friend Valiant, and may I wish you every happiness."

"Thank . . . you," Gytha replied in a low voice.

"I want to tell you . . ." Lord Locke began.

Before he could say any more, the door opened.

The most beautiful woman Gytha could ever have imagined came in.

Her gown was fantastic.

At the same time its low décolletage and almost transparent skirt seemed outrageous.

The jewels she wore looked worth a King's ransom.

The woman walked with a feline grace towards Lord Locke and slipped her arm through his.

"I was told you wanted to see me particularly, Valiant," she said in a voice of velvet, "and I thought that meant we should be alone."

"I asked you to come to see me here before you went into the Salon," Lord Locke replied, "because, Zuleika, I wanted to let you into a secret which will not be made public for some time."

"A secret? What secret could you have from me, my dearest?" Zuleika asked.

"I want you," Lord Locke replied slowly, "to meet my *fiancée*, Miss Gytha Sullivan!"

For a moment there was a strange silence.

Gytha felt as if everybody in the room had been turned to stone.

Then with what she knew was an effort, Lord Locke added:

"Gytha, this is a very old friend of mine, the Princess Zuleika El Saladin, who I wanted to be one of the first to congratulate us, together with my other old friend, Perry, whom you met this afternoon."

Again there was that strange, pregnant silence.

Then as Gytha looked at the Princess she saw her dark eyes narrow.

There was an expression on her face that was not only one of surprise.

It also, Gytha thought, betokened danger and what she could describe to herself only as evil.

Then in dulcet tones which were quite obviously insincere Zuleika said:

"This is a surprise, a very great surprise, and of course I must wish you good fortune and that you will be happy with such a charming if very young—bride."

As she spoke Gytha knew the Princess was an unrelenting, implacable enemy.

As dangerous as a cobra.

chapter four

WHEN she awoke, Gytha lay thinking of what had happened the previous evening.

It had been very exciting.

Dinner had been in a beautiful Dining-Room decorated with Adam furniture.

Its alcoves were filled with statues of Greek gods.

The room was as unexpected as the conversation.

Gytha had thought she would feel gauche and countrified.

She expected to have nothing to say to Lord Locke's fashionable friends.

Perry, however, was on her left.

He immediately began to talk of horses, while Lord Locke on her other side soon joined in.

Because the only interest available to Gytha was horses, she not only loved them but read about them.

She followed all the races which were reported in the newspapers.

She had learnt the history of racing through the ages.

This was easy because her father's Library had been moved to her grandfather's house.

It contained a great number of books on breeding.

There were others on the development of carriage horses ever since the chariot-races in Roman times.

She therefore found it easy to talk about form.

She knew which important races had been won by Lord Locke.

She began to understand how preoccupied every man at the party was with this particular sport.

Gytha's reading had not been confined only to one subject.

Her mother had been extremely interested in the religions of the East.

Her maternal grandfather, whom she had known only when she was a child, had been a great traveller.

He had visited countries where few white men had ever set foot.

He had written down his adventures.

He had also written of his impressions and everything he found of interest on his travels.

Because his hand-writing was sometimes almost illegible, Gytha had copied it out in her clear, flowing hand.

She enjoyed doing it because every word she transcribed seemed so enthralling.

She was also specially interested in the war with Napoleon.

This was because her father had been in the Army.

She had read every book which had been published about the Duke of Wellington and Napoleon Bonaparte.

She had a great deal to talk about to her male dinner-companions.

Until dinner was over she never gave a thought to herself or to her appearance.

Nor did she think that she might be expected to be shy.

But when the ladies left the gentlemen to their port

and proceeded to the Salon, she became acutely aware of the Princess Zuleika.

Lord Locke had made one thing clear before dinner.

Since they were short of ladies, those that were there would have to be dispersed round the table.

He asked the Princess to sit at the far end opposite him.

Her dark eyes flashed.

It was as if she realised he was deliberately excluding her from being close to him.

But she could not refuse.

Instead, Lord Locke had on one side the very attractive second wife of the Lord Lieutenant.

She was trying desperately after a childless marriage to beget an heir.

It was obvious what many of the other guests who came from neighbouring houses thought strange.

It was that Gytha, a young girl, was sitting next to their host.

She knew perceptively the reason he had put her there.

It was that he wanted to impress on Princess Zuleika the importance of the secret he had confided to her.

Gytha was not so foolish that she did not realise that the Princess was in love with Lord Locke.

She obviously considered that he belonged to her exclusively.

She told herself humbly that he was prepared to help her as a debt of gratitude.

Her father had saved his life.

But his affections could not fail to be captivated by the exotic beauty of the Princess.

She thought therefore it was extremely brave and

very chivalrous of him to protect her.

It was at the expense of making things uncomfortable for himself.

She only wondered why, since they were such good friends, he did not tell the Princess the truth.

Then she thought he probably was wise not to confide in anybody.

Not even so close a friend as the Princess must know there was anything unusual about their engagement.

No woman could resist passing on so sensational a secret to somebody else.

No woman could really be trusted not to make an intriguing story out of Lord Locke paying a debt of honour in such an unusual manner.

With a little sigh of relief Gytha thought that no one would know the truth until her grandfather died.

This meant that she would be safe.

At least, until that happened, from Vincent and Jonathan.

Another idea had passed through her mind.

When her Cousins learnt that she was no longer protected by Lord Locke, they might pursue her for her fortune.

By that time, however, she was sure she could have made plans.

She would be with somebody who could deal with fortune-hunters.

Perhaps also with other pursuers not so obviously unpleasant.

When the ladies reached the Salon, where they had met before dinner, the Princess spoke to Gytha for the first time.

She had deliberately ignored her when Lord Locke had taken Gytha and Perry into the Salon.

Quite a number of the house-party were already assembled there.

There were two extremely attractive ladies, who were introduced to Gytha as Lady Compton and the Countess Blackstone.

They had looked her up and down in an almost contemptuous manner.

They obviously considered her a country bumpkin of no consequence.

After the introduction they made no further effort to speak to her again.

The guests from neighbouring houses expressed their surprise at seeing Gytha.

Since her mother's death she had been living in virtual seclusion alone with her grandfather.

She was therefore almost a stranger to them.

Only Laky Wakefield, who was slightly older than the others, said with undisguised candour:

"I never thought after all the animosity between your grandfather and the old Lord Locke that I would see you here at the Hall."

"I am a little surprised myself to be here," Gytha replied. "But happily, Grandpapa has agreed that it is ridiculous to go on fighting over Monk's Wood."

"I am glad to hear that," Lady Wakefield said, "but if the feud is now over, what shall we find to talk about in the County?"

It was certain, Gytha thought, to be a topic of conversation at least for the moment!

She could hear Lady Wakefield later telling two of Lord Locke's guests that the two old gentlemen had raged at each other for years.

She reiterated how amusing everybody had found their anger and their hatred of each other.

As they returned to the Salon after dinner, Gytha thought it would be a good idea to talk to Lady Wakefield.

She was just moving towards her when the Princess came up to her.

She could no longer disguise the anger and hatred in her eyes.

Her red lips twisted in an ugly manner as she asked:

"Where have you come from, Miss Sullivan, and why had I not heard of you before?"

"I live next door," Gytha explained. "My grandfather's estate and Lord Locke's march with each other."

"And you really think you are fit to marry anyone so handsome and so attractive as His Lordship?"

She seemed almost to spit the words at Gytha.

She felt her heart beginning to beat tumultuously.

At the same time she managed to say quietly:

"As you have been informed, any arrangement there is between us is a secret."

She lowered her voice as she spoke.

It indicated that she thought the Princess was being indiscreet.

For the moment the other ladies could not overhear their conversation.

The Princess came a step nearer to her as she said:

"If you think you can take him away from me, you are mistaken! He is mine, do you understand? Mine! If you try to come between us you will be sorry—very sorry—for your presumption!"

The words conveyed an undisguised threat.

They were spoken with a slight accent that could make the Princess's voice seductively alluring but now undeniably frightening.

Gytha felt herself tremble.

Then she told herself she need not be afraid of this woman.

The Princess was, to say the least of it, behaving in a very unladylike manner.

Lifting her chin, Gytha deliberately walked past her and across the room to where Lady Wakefield was sitting on a comfortable sofa.

As she did so she was conscious that the Princess's animosity vibrated after her.

It was almost as if she had fired a pistol at her from behind.

Lady Wakefield was only too willing to talk to Gytha.

"Finding you here tonight, I feel ashamed that I have not invited you to my house since your mother's death, but to tell you the truth, we are all a little afraid of your grandfather and realise that he does not welcome visitors."

"Grandpapa is very ill," Gytha said, "and of course I was in mourning until the summer."

"Now you are going out and about again," Lady Wakefield continued. "You must come to luncheon with me. In two weeks time I will have some young people staying with me, so I will give a dinner-party and you can dance afterwards."

She paused and added:

"Perhaps you can persuade Lord Locke to join us."

There was an expression in Lady Wakefield's eyes which told Gytha she would consider it a "feather in her cap" to have Lord Locke as her guest.

After a moment, as if she could not retain her curiosity any longer, Lady Wakefield asked:

"Have you known Lord Locke for long? If you have,

it seems extraordinary you should have met, considering the warfare that has raged between your two families for so long."

Gytha was ready for this question, and she said:

"We both have a great love of horses."

"Oh, of course!" Lake Wakefield said. "You must have met out hunting, and who could resist admiring the animals from the Locke stables, which are superb."

By the time the gentlemen had joined the ladies, Gytha had managed to evade many questions from other ladies in the party.

These included the Lord Lieutenant's wife, who obviously had found Lord Locke extremely attractive.

She had made the very most of being beside him at dinner.

All the time, however, Gytha was conscious of the Princess's hatred.

Because she was very sensitive to other people's vibrations, she could feel the Princess's eyes on her.

She thought they were like burning embers searing their way into her flesh.

She thought it was time for her to leave.

Lord Locke escorted her to the door, saying in a voice that only she could hear:

"You were splendid! I have my house-party to look after tomorrow, but I will call on you sometime during the afternoon."

Gytha smiled at him.

Driving home in his comfortable carriage, she thought how wonderful he was.

It was marvellous of him to have agreed to her suggestion of an engagement.

"I am sure it was you, Papa, who put the idea into

my mind," she said in her heart, "and persuaded Lord Locke to agree."

She paused before, with a touch of fear in her voice, she went on:

"Now I have only to convince Vincent and Jonathan that they have no hope of getting hold of Grandpapa's money through me!"

She had the idea that it would not be as easy as it sounded.

But as she went to sleep she tried to think only of Lord Locke.

She could see him riding his magnificent black stallion over the jumps.

She wanted to thank him for his kindness in rescuing her from her cousins.

*　　*　　*

As she got up and dressed she only wished Lord Locke could be with her.

She knew she would be frightened when she told Vincent and Jonathan that she was engaged to him.

She came downstairs and the house seemed very dark and silent—especially after the chatter and laughter at Locke Hall.

Heavy oak panelling covered most of the walls.

The large rather ugly mahogany furniture, and the portraits of her ancestors, made everything seem gloomy.

Heavily tasselled curtains prevented the sunshine from coming in through the windows.

In contrast, the rooms at Locke Hall had been bright with the light.

Not only from the crystal chandeliers, but from the

white walls picked out in gold.

The painted ceilings, decorated as Gytha had learned by famous Italian artists, were very different from anything she had seen before.

Everything about Lord Locke was unusual, she told herself.

He was as magnificent as his horses.

Then she saw her Cousin Vincent coming in through the front-door.

He must have been very eager to obey her grandfather's summons.

He had therefore stayed overnight with a friend, or else at a Posting Inn.

He was dressed as usual in a dandified manner.

His coat was cut in an exaggerated style, the points of his collar above his white cravat too high!

She looked at his thin, tight lips, his large, supercilious nose.

His small pig-like eyes were too close together.

She felt revolted by him.

"Good morning, Gytha!" he said in the lofty voice in which he habitually addressed her. "I suppose Uncle Robert has not yet come downstairs."

"No, it is too early for him," Gytha replied, "and I was, in fact, expecting you later."

"I wish to speak to you alone."

Gytha knew this meant that he intended to propose to her.

"I am afraid I have something important to do," she said swiftly, "so perhaps we can talk when Grandpapa comes down."

"I said I wish to speak to you alone," Vincent said insistently. "Come into the Drawing-Room."

Gytha tried to think of some excuse.

Because she was so much younger than her cousins, she was used to obeying them.

While she was frantically trying to find words to excuse herself, Vincent took her by the arm.

He led her firmly across the hall and into the Drawing-Room, with its stiff furniture upholstered in dark damask.

It had often made Gytha think it looked like a funeral-parlour.

He shut the door behind him and Gytha said quickly:

"I wanted to wait until Grandpapa came down before I told you my news."

"News? What news?"

He walked towards the fireplace as he spoke.

He was thinking, Gytha was convinced, that he cut a very fine figure of a man.

His champagne-coloured breeches fitted closely to his skin, his polished Hessian boots had two gold tassels dangling from the fronts of them.

He turned round as he reached the fireplace.

He surveyed her almost, she thought, like a Sultan inspecting a new addition to his Harem.

She could read his thoughts.

She was sure he was thinking that she was not in any way to his taste.

Nevertheless the fortune she would inherit from her grandfather would cover a multitude of defects.

"I would rather Grandpapa were here to tell you," Gytha said in answer to his last question.

She felt her voice sounded small and ineffectual.

She was sure she herself looked no more convincing.

"What can Uncle Robert have to tell me that you cannot relate to me first?" Vincent asked. "In fact, I would rather be prepared."

Gytha did not speak.

After a moment he said in an irritated tone:

"Stop behaving in this mousy fashion and explain to me what has happened since I was last here, although I cannot imagine it is of any particular import."

"Only to me."

"Then what is it?"

She drew a deep breath.

"I am . . . engaged to be . . . married to . . . Lord Locke!"

For a moment Vincent just stared at her with his piggy eyes.

Then he said:

"I do not believe it! Uncle Robert would never countenance an alliance with the Lockes with whom we have been on bad terms for over twenty-five years."

"Grandpapa has agreed that we . . . should be engaged . . . but it must not be . . . announced until he knows Lord Locke . . . better."

"I have never heard anything so outrageous!" Vincent said. "How dare you presume to make friends with a family which has insulted us and deliberately tried to steal one of our woods!"

"Lord Locke has now relinquished all claims to the wood . . . and has promised Grandpapa that it will be erased from every map on the Locke estate."

"It should never have been included on them in the first place," Vincent snapped, "but that is immaterial. Uncle Robert must be deranged if he has agreed to this ridiculous marriage, and it is something I shall fight with every means in my power."

"Why should you . . . want to do . . . that?" Gytha asked in pretended innocence.

"Because I intend to marry you myself!" Vincent replied. "You need somebody to look after you now that both your parents are dead, and as my wife you will have my protection, and what is more, my name."

"Which is mine already," Gytha pointed out. "Although it is very kind of you to ask me to be your wife, Vincent, I am afraid you are . . . too late. I have already given . . . my promise to . . . Lord Locke."

She found herself growing braver as she spoke.

But she was not prepared for the fury which seemed to contort Vincent's face as he shouted:

"You shall not marry Lord Locke! I forbid it! Do you hear? I absolutely forbid it!"

His voice seemed to echo round the room.

He looked so frightening that Gytha, who had not sat down, took several steps backwards.

She was afraid that he would strike her.

Just then the door opened and Sir Robert, wheeled by Dobson, came into the room.

"What is all this noise?" he demanded.

Dobson moved the wheelchair until he stopped in front of Vincent.

"You can leave us, Dobson," Sir Robert said.

The valet walked slowly away as if he was reluctant to miss what looked like a promising scene.

Sir Robert looked from Gytha to his nephew, then he asked sharply:

"What is all this noise? What do you mean by shouting at Gytha?"

"If I was shouting," Vincent replied in a different tone of voice from the one he had used before, "it is because I am so surprised, Uncle Robert, not to say astounded at your giving your permission for Gytha to marry a man whom I have always considered an enemy."

"What you consider or do not consider is of no consequence," Sir Robert said. "Locke may be his father's son, but he has proved himself to be a good soldier and has several medals to prove it."

The way he spoke told Gytha she had been right.

Her grandfather had always resented the fact that neither Vincent nor Jonathan had taken an active part in the war.

"I cannot understand," Vincent said after a moment, "why the fact that he is a good soldier should entitle him to marry Gytha. Furthermore, I always believed that you intended her to marry either me or Jonathan."

"Well, I have changed my mind," Sir Robert said, "and if Gytha marries Locke, you will have to find another heiress to pay for your extravagant ways."

"I cannot see why I should do anything of the sort!" Vincent said angrily. "I shall marry Gytha, and whatever you may say now, you led me to believe that such an idea met with your approval."

"I will leave my money where I like," Sir Robert said fiercely. "I made it without any help from a lot of carping relatives, and why should your only contribution be in helping to spend it?"

"I think that is unfair . . ." Vincent began.

At that moment the door opened and Jonathan came in.

He was looking, Gytha thought, more unpleasant than usual.

With an ingratiating smile on his face he reminded her of a Cheshire cat which had eaten too much cream.

He tried to dress smartly in the same fashion as his brother.

Because he was shorter and more stouter, nothing looked right on him.

Already, after what had been only quite a short journey, his cravat looked crumpled.

His polished boots were obviously smudged.

Gytha had always thought, too, that he was not as clean as Vincent.

His hands were not only wet and clammy but often unwashed.

"Good morning, Uncle Robert!" he said in the silky, smarmy tones he always used to the old man. "How delightful to see you again, and in such good health!"

"I am damned ill," Sir Robert replied, "and you know it!"

"Good morning, Gytha!" Jonathan said. "How pretty you look! As fresh as the flowers in Springtime, as the poets say!"

"Stop babbling," Vincent commanded. "Listen to what has happened, and see if you do not consider that Uncle Robert has treated us shabbily."

Jonathan gave Sir Robert a glance that was very much sharper than the silken tones of his tongue before he asked:

"What can have happened in this delightful house where I always feel so happy and at home?"

"You may as well enjoy it while you can," Vincent said. "Gytha considers herself engaged to that outsider Locke, to whom no Sullivan has spoken for over twenty-five years!"

"Lord Locke?" Jonathan asked in astonishment.

"Who else do you think I am talking about?" Vincent demanded sharply. "Just tell Uncle Robert it is something he should not allow and we will not permit."

"Are you insinuating that I am becoming senile in my old age?" Sir Robert enquired in a voice of thunder. "*You* will not permit? You who have done nothing since leaving school but beg first from your father, then from me, for money."

He paused before he went on furiously:

"You do not suppose I am not aware that the only reason why you came charging down here a short time ago was when it suddenly struck you that I might make Gytha my heir rather than either of you!"

"I understood you wanted one of us to marry Gytha," Vincent retorted, "and thus keep the money in the family and ensure that a Sullivan inherited the estate."

"Yes, that is what I thought too," Jonathan piped up. "I thought either of us could marry dear Gytha, and I hoped the sweet little thing would favour me."

He gave Gytha a look which made her shudder.

Instinctively she moved nearer to her grandfather as if for protection.

"Well, you have both of you backed the wrong horse," Sir Robert said. "Gytha intends to marry Lord Locke, and although I do not like the stable from which he comes, at least he is not hanging around after my money like you two!"

"Are you seriously telling us, Uncle Robert," Vincent cried, "that you are not only willing to allow this marriage so that Gytha will be a Locke rather than a Sullivan, but that you do not intend to provide for Jonathan or me?"

"Provide? You are provided for already. Your father left you all he had, and if you do not think that is enough, then that is no concern of mine!"

"But, Uncle Robert, we shall be impoverished!" Jonathan whined. "How can you bear to think of your nephews living in poverty and having to sponge off our friends?"

"What is the difference from your sponging off me?"

Sir Robert asked. "You do not think I have not seen through your efforts to soft-soap me, young man, or your brother's insistence that 'blood is thicker than water'?"

He waited for a reply.

When there was only an embarrassed silence he continued:

"I am no fool, and both of you are fortune-hunters. Now you can find a fortune elsewhere. Gytha will have everything I possess, and if she allows you to live in the family house, you will be lucky."

"But we have no money with which to keep it up!" Jonathan cried.

"Find some! Make some! Stir yourselves for a change!" Sir Robert shouted. "How do you think I made money? By using my brains—not by relying on my relations who were all as half-witted as you are!"

His voice thundered out as he added:

"Half-witted nincompoops without a brain between the two of you! I will not have my money—my money —frittered away, and at least Locke understands horse-flesh. I would not trust either of you to buy a mule."

The old man's face had become crimson as he ranted at them.

Suddenly his chin dropped on his chest.

He seemed to be having difficulty in breathing.

It was something that had happened to him before.

Gytha knew the doctor had left him a special drug to take when this occurred.

Hastily she ran to the door.

As she expected, Dobson was just outside.

She was certain even as she turned the handle that he rose to his feet.

He had been listening at the key-hole.

"The Master's drops, quickly!" she said.

The valet hurried into the room.

He took a small bottle from his pocket as he did so.

He picked up a glass from the grog-tray.

Half-filling it with water, he measured some drops into it.

Then he tipped it into Sir Robert's mouth.

There was silence while everybody waited for the drops to take effect.

But Sir Robert still lay back with his eyes closed.

Dobson turned his chair round to face the door.

"You're killing him—that's what you're doing!" he said in a rude voice to Vincent.

Then he wheeled his Master from the Drawing-Room.

He left the three cousins staring after him.

It was Vincent who spoke first.

"Now we have lost everything."

"Is there any chance of his changing his Will?" Jonathan enquired.

"I doubt it," Vincent replied, "but we could contest it once he is dead. Make no mistake, Gytha. If you have persuaded him to leave you everything, we will fight you in the Courts, you may be sure of that!"

She thought that both her cousins were heartless and despicable!

After a moment Gytha said quietly:

"I shall let Lord Locke look after my interests."

"Now, look here, my girl," Vincent said, "you listen to us."

"I am not going to listen to you," Gytha retorted. "You both make me feel sick by the way you behave. I have always known you were utterly contemptible."

Her voice rose as she continued:

"You came to see Grandpapa only because you wanted his money. Now you have told the truth, and I hope I never see either of you again!"

She walked out of the room as she spoke.

As she was shutting the door she heard Jonathan say:

"See what you have done, Vincent! We have somehow got to make her change her mind!"

'That is something they will never be able to do,' Gytha thought.

She ran upstairs to find out how her grandfather was.

* * *

Gytha learned that Vincent and Jonathan were staying to luncheon.

She therefore ordered her own meal to be brought upstairs in her sitting-room.

She ate alone.

Then because she wanted to avoid further altercation with her cousins, she walked along the drive.

She was hoping to intercept Lord Locke if he came to call as he had promised.

She looked between the oak trees.

At last she saw him in the distance and felt a sudden leap of her heart.

As he drew nearer she could see the jaunty angle at which he wore his high hat.

The way he was riding the same black stallion that had won the Steeple-chase.

She knew that no man could look more handsome or ride with an expertise which would have delighted her father.

He saw her and swept off his hat as he drew his horse to a standstill.

"Good afternoon, Gytha! Have you come to meet me?"

"Yes, I came to tell you before you reached the house that . . . both my . . . cousins are . . . there."

The way she spoke made him ask sharply:

"What has happened?"

"I told them . . . we were . . . engaged," Gytha said with a tremor in her voice. "Then Grandpapa came down . . . and there was a . . . terrible row. It . . . upset Grandpapa so that he had a kind of seizure and had to be . . . taken to bed."

She paused before she added:

"Vincent and Jonathan have threatened that if Grandpapa leaves everything to me, they will contest the Will."

"That is what I might have expected!" Lord Locke exclaimed.

He dismounted and stood beside her.

As he looked down at her he realised that her face was very pale.

Her eyes were larger and more frightened than they had been yesterday.

"What do you want me to do?" he asked.

"Is it too much to ask of you to meet them? I do think, if they see you, they will . . . realise what I said is . . . serious and there is . . . nothing they can do . . . about it."

"I doubt if meeting me will make them change their minds about contesting the Will," Lord Locke said, "but I am perfectly prepared to do anything you want of me."

"Thank you," Gytha said.

They walked slowly down the drive.

Lord Locke led Hercules, until a groom standing outside the house saw them.

He hurried to the horse's head.

Then as they climbed the steps and entered the house Lord Locke was aware that Gytha was really frightened.

He thought it outrageous that she should be subjected to such strain when she was so young and alone.

"Surely," he asked as they walked through the hall, "there is some relative, an older woman, you could ask to come to stay with you?"

"I doubt if anyone would put up with Grandpapa for long," Gytha said ruefully, "and he is very difficult about having strangers in the house."

She opened the door of the Drawing-Room.

As she expected, Vincent and his brother were sitting in front of the fire.

They were obviously discussing what they could do about the new situation.

She supposed they were waiting.

They were hoping to see Sir Robert again and would try to make him change his mind.

Gytha was quite certain that Dobson would not allow anyone near Sir Robert.

He would insist on his resting quietly without being disturbed.

Now although she was frightened, she managed to appear at her ease.

She walked down the room with Lord Locke beside her.

Reluctantly Vincent and Jonathan rose to their feet.

"I thought, Cousin Vincent," she said, "you would like to meet my *fiancé*, Lord Locke."

In his fury, Vincent's eyebrows seemed almost to meet across the bridge of his nose as he replied:

"I never expected to encounter Your Lordship in this house."

"It is rather a surprise to find myself here," Lord Locke replied. "But surely we are all intelligent enough to realise that this ridiculous feud should come to an end and what better way to end it than that our two families should be united in marriage?"

He was amused by the fury on Vincent's face as he spoke.

Jonathan looked as if he were going to burst into tears.

"I consider," Vincent said ponderously, "that you must have taken advantage of my cousin in persuading her to marry you, even if you were not aware that my uncle always intended she should marry either my brother or me."

"I can understand your feelings," Lord Locke said, "but as Gytha has made it clear that she prefers me, I hope you will both be sporting enough to wish us happiness and show no ill-feeling."

"Pretty words!" Vincent sneered. "The fact remains that you, or rather Gytha, are deliberately robbing us of our inheritance, to which we are entitled as Sullivans."

"Having met your uncle," Lord Locke replied, "I am convinced that he is perfectly capable of making up his own mind as to who shall benefit under his Will. Gytha has not influenced him in the way you are insinuating."

"I have my own opinion about that," Vincent replied. "I am convinced I can find witnesses to prove not only that my uncle is deranged, but that he had been illegally persuaded into making a Will entirely in his granddaughter's favour."

"That, of course, will be for the Courts to decide," Lord Locke replied. "I shall certainly employ learned Counsel to represent my *fiancée* and make quite certain she is not deprived of anything to which she is entitled."

He turned as he spoke to Gytha, saying as he did so:

"I think, my dear, no good can come of our arguing further with these gentlemen. Just leave all your problems in my hands, as I do not wish you to be troubled by them."

"Thank . . . you," Gytha replied.

The look in her eyes was more expressive than her words.

Lord Locke drew her from the room.

As they moved down the passage towards the Study she said:

"Thank you . . . thank you! How can you be so . . . wonderful? I am sure now Vincent and Jonathan will think . . . twice before they . . . upset Grandpapa again, or start any . . . proceedings . . . against me."

"They cannot do that anyhow until your grandfather is dead."

Gytha drew in her breath.

She suddenly realised that once her grandfather was dead, their supposed engagement would come to an end.

He would not be there to fight her battles for her and protect her.

Lord Locke did not seem to notice the drab appearance of the Study.

He stood in front of the fire, saying:

"Do not worry yourself. I am quite certain your Cousin Vincent will realise that going to law with a very slim chance of winning a long-drawn-out case would cost a great deal of money—which I understand he does not possess."

He paused before he continued:

"In his own interests it would be far better for him to make himself pleasant to you in the hope that you will give him and his brother a small allowance. If your grandfather's wealth is as great as you suspect, that will be quite easy to do."

"Yes, of course," Gytha said, "and I would be quite willing to help them. But I think they would want much more than a little—in fact, practically everything I possess."

"That they certainly must not have!" Lord Locke said firmly.

He looked to where she was sitting, small and despondent.

Once again he thought her golden hair was like the sunshine.

"Surely," he asked, "as I suggested before, you should have somebody here with you. After all, your grandfather is very ill, and cannot want you with him every hour of the day. At least you would have somebody to talk to."

"I would like that," Gytha said, "but I know it would annoy Grandpapa very much if I engaged anyone without his permission. In any case, I have no idea who I could ask to come here. They would find it very dull!"

"But you are prepared to put up with it?"

Gytha smiled.

"It is impossible for me to go away, and anyway, I have nowhere to go and no money."

"I do not believe I have ever met anybody with so many difficulties in her life all at once!" Lord Locke smiled. "I suppose it is impossible for me to suggest that you come to stay in my house for a few days?"

He saw Gytha's eyes light up. Then she said:

"That is something I would . . . love to do . . . but perhaps it would . . . upset your . . . friend."

Lord Locke knew to which particular friend she was referring.

Before he could speak she went on:

"Anyway, I am sure it would upset Grandpapa. But perhaps you could ask me to luncheon or dinner another day. That would be very exciting for me."

"You will be welcome any time," Lord Locke replied, "and as my house-party are leaving tomorrow morning, I suggest you come over to luncheon, and again in the evening."

"Thank you. It is very kind of you."

"I must leave you now, and do not allow yourself to be upset by your cousins."

"I will try not to see them," Gytha answered. "I had luncheon upstairs today and will stay there as long as they remain. I am hoping they will leave before dinner."

"Then I will see you tomorrow for luncheon," Lord Locke said. "Take care of yourself, Gytha, and if at any time you need me, send a groom with a message and I will come to you immediately."

"Thank you . . . thank you!" Gytha said again.

He knew her gratitude came from her heart.

She walked with him to the front-door.

As he mounted his horse he swept off his hat.

She thought it was a courtly gesture.

He rode away.

She watched him until he was out of sight.

She would have been flattered if she had known that as Lord Locke rode across the Park, he was thinking that standing on the top of the steps she looked very small, frail, and insecure.

It was almost as if the huge, ugly house were menacing her and she might be crushed by the weight of it.

Then he told himself he was being absurdly imaginative.

At the same time, he was doing the best he could to repay the debt he owed to her father.

chapter five

LORD Locke had passed a restless night.

To begin with, he was aware that Zuleika was determined to have a scene with him sooner or later.

He had every intention of avoiding it.

It was two o'clock in the morning when the house-party finally went up to bed.

They had gambled for very high stakes at the card-tables.

Lord Locke, instead of going to his own room, went into Perry's.

"What is the situation now?" Perry asked.

He was the only person to whom Lord Locke had told the truth about his alleged engagement to Gytha.

After she had been to dinner, Perry had sung her praises loudly and sincerely.

"She is beautiful and she is intelligent," he said, "and although she needs dressing up to compete with the Beauties of St. James's, she is, in my opinion, an exceptional young woman."

Lord Locke was hardly listening.

Now as he entered his friend's room Perry knew by the expression on his face what was worrying him.

"I suppose there is nothing you can do about

Zuleika," he said cheerily, "except hope that tomorrow comes quickly."

"She has been trying all day to get me alone," Lord Locke replied, "and I suspect she reckons that now the hour has come."

"Lock your door, old man!" Perry teased.

"It goes against the grain to do anything that makes me feel like a young housemaid being pursued by a lecherous master," Lord Locke said sharply.

Perry laughed but Lord Locke went on:

"I suppose I have no alternative, except to listen to what she is longing to say to me."

"I would advise you not to do that," Perry said. "You know these Eastern people—very long-winded when it comes to a grievance."

Lord Locke, watching his friend as he took off his well-tied cravat, knew he was speaking the truth.

"I have a feeling that Zuleika is going to be very difficult," he said reflectively as if he were talking to himself.

"I will wager that is the understatement of the year!" Perry replied. "I always thought she was bad news from the first moment you produced her."

Lord Locke sighed.

"I think she produced herself, or rather, attached herself to me."

"And now," Perry remarked, "she is like a piece of clinging ivy, and if you pull off one piece, another sticks on."

"You are not being much help," Lord Locke complained.

"If you are asking for advice," Perry replied, "the best thing you can do is to sleep in a different room. Heaven knows, you have enough of them!"

"That is the first intelligent thing you have said so far."

Lord Locke rose as he spoke and walked towards the door.

"Goodnight, Perry. Ride with me before breakfast and then help me speed the parting guests. I have no wish for Zuleika to remain behind."

"That is your job, old boy, not mine!" Perry said blithely.

Lord Locke went to his own room, but before he rang for his valet he had an idea.

He took a beautiful arrangement of chrysanthemums out of a vase which stood on one of the chest-of-drawers.

He pushed the flowers as high as he could up the chimney, then put two fresh logs on the fire.

It was only a few minutes before smoke began to ooze out into the room.

He rang the bell for his valet.

Walters, an athletic little man who had served with him in his Regiment, came hurrying at the summons.

Having opened the door, he looked with surprise at the smoke.

"The fire's smoking, M'Lord," he exclaimed unnecessarily, "and the chimney-sweep were 'ere only ten days ago. It's a disgrace—that's what it is!"

"I agree with you," Lord Locke replied, "and as I have no intention of choking myself, you had better take my night clothes to the Marlborough Room. I imagine the bed is made up!"

"O'course, M'Lord. Th' rooms on this floor are always ready in case Your Lordship 'as some unexpected guests."

"Very well, that is where I will sleep."

He walked quickly down the corridor.

He was hoping that Zuleika, whose room was only a few doors away from his, would not be aware that he had moved.

Then when he was undressed and in bed, he was strangely not thinking of the trouble Zuleika was likely to be.

Instead, he was considering what he should do about Gytha.

He could quite understand her dislike of Vincent, whom he recognised as a "fop" of the worst description.

Jonathan, he thought, was equally unpleasant.

"I shall have to do something about her," he decided.

He had, however, no notion for the moment what it could be.

He found it difficult to sleep, tossing and turning.

He was considering the unpleasant possibility of the Sullivan brothers bringing a case against Gytha after her grandfather's death.

He knew that however much he might try to avoid it, he would inevitably be involved.

"Somebody should look after her," he said into the darkness.

Then he found himself remembering how kind and understanding her father had been.

He was like a father to all the young officers when they joined the Regiment in France and had their first baptism of fire.

Before he went to sleep, Lord Locke told himself he should have got in touch with Gytha and her mother as soon as the war was over.

He tried to excuse his negligence that first he had been in the Army of Occupation and then in London.

It was when he had come to the country that he remembered the age-old battle of his family with the Sullivans.

If Colonel Sullivan had lived, he would now be Sir Robert's heir rather than Gytha.

He knew what difficulties would beset a young girl who was an heiress.

Her fortune was bound to attract the worst type of men.

'No one, in fact, could be worse,' he thought, 'than her two cousins!'

Whatever they were like, he was quite certain Gytha would be unable to defend herself.

How could she cope with the type of situation which would be inevitable?

She was not only rich, but also very lovely.

He was thinking of her beauty as he finally fell asleep.

When he awoke in the morning he had the strange feeling that she needed him.

He told himself he was just being imaginative.

After riding as arranged with Perry, he returned to eat a hearty breakfast before any of the other male members of his party appeared.

"I have enjoyed every minute of my visit, Valiant," one of them said a little later. "I hope I have not 'blotted my copy-book' and you will ask me again."

He spoke as if this were unlikely.

Lord Locke could only reply:

"Of course. I shall look forward to entertaining you again before Christmas."

When breakfast was finished, the gentlemen left the Dining-Room.

Bates came to Lord Locke's side to say in a low voice:

"Her Highness wished to see Your Lordship immediately."

"Where?" Lord Locke asked.

"In Her Highness's *Boudoir*."

"Inform Her Highness that as I am engaged in seeing off the guests who are leaving early, it is impossible for me to comply with her request."

He paused before he added:

"Make it clear, Bates, that the carriage which will take her back to London has been ordered for eleven o'clock."

Bates started to climb the stairs.

Lord Locke walked into the Library.

Perry and two of his other friends were inevitably talking about horses.

He joined in their conversation until the door opened.

Zuleika, looking extremely attractive and flamboyant in a bonnet covered with crimson feathers, swept into the room.

As the gentlemen rose to their feet she said:

"I have to talk to you, Valiant."

Before Lord Locke could reply she gave Perry and the other two men in the room her most bewitching smile.

"I know you dear men will understand," she said, "that I have something of great importance to tell our wonderful host. As it is a secret, I must ask you to be kind and understanding enough to leave us alone."

There was nothing the three men could do but comply.

Perry gave Lord Locke a meaningful glance as he walked towards the door.

As soon as it had shut behind them, Zuleika ran to Lord Locke, throwing herself against him and asked:

"How can you be so cruel, so unkind to me, when I love you? Oh, Valiant, how much I love you!"

Lord Locke did not put his arms around her, he merely said:

"I think, Zuleika, we are both adult and sensible enough to realise that what one might call the 'fires of love' are not so bright as they have been in the past."

He sounded very sincere as he continued:

"I can therefore only say how grateful I am for the happiness you have given me, and when I return to London I will send you a present to express my gratitude."

Zuleika did not move.

But he felt her sensuous body stiffen against him.

"Are you trying to throw me off?" Zuleika asked. "To commit me to a hopelessness that will make me utterly and completely miserable?"

"I hope you will be none of those things," Lord Locke said.

Zuleika's eyes looked up at him beseechingly as she said:

"I waited for you last night."

"I was tired."

"I have never before known you tired! Can you really prefer that milk-faced girl to me?"

Then with a change of tone she said fiercely:

"How can you be so foolish as to think you can forget the burning passion we have shared together, and the ecstasy we have given each other."

Her voice rose to a crescendo as she cried:

"No, no! Only I can give you what you need! Only I can make you know the joy of requited desire."

Now her eyes were flashing, her breasts were heaving.

The words seemed to burst from her red lips as if she could no longer control them.

"Now, listen, Zuleika . . ." began Lord Locke.

"I will not listen! You will listen to me! You are mine—do you hear me?—mine, Valiant, and I will allow no stupid country girl to come between us!"

She made a pathetic little sound and held herself closer against him as she said:

"Marry me! I will make you very happy and be a wife to be proud of!"

"I am sorry, Zuleika," Lord Locke said, "but as I told you yesterday, I am engaged to Miss Gytha Sullivan, and our betrothal is as binding as if we were already married."

He spoke firmly, with authority.

The men who had served under him had recognised this as final and admitting no argument.

For a moment there was silence.

Then as Zuleika moved a little away from him she said:

"Very well then—you and this country-bumpkin will suffer for this! I will not be treated in such a manner by any man without revenging myself."

Her green eyes narrowed.

"Remember that, Valiant! What is more, the day will come when you will return to me, when you know there is no one else who can arouse in you the fires of desire as I can."

She seemed to hiss the last words.

It was as if they came from a snake rather than from a woman.

Then she turned and walked slowly from the room.

She glided across the carpet in a sinuous manner

which seemed to emphasize the threats she had just uttered.

Lord Locke did not move.

Only when he was alone did he give a sigh of relief and hope that Zuleika would leave without his having to see her again.

Some of the other members of the party, however, did not arrange to depart until after luncheon.

Lord Locke was having a glass of champagne with them in the Salon.

It was then he remembered that thinking he and Perry would be alone, he had invited Gytha both to luncheon and to dinner.

He was just about to tell Bates he was expecting her when a note arrived.

When it was handed to him on a silver salver he found it was from Gytha.

He read:

My Lord:

Please excuse me from accepting your kind invitation for luncheon and dinner today, but Grandpapa is not well, and the doctors say he must be kept very quiet and that the only person to see him is myself.

You will therefore understand that I must be on call if he needs me.

Thank you for coming over yesterday, and I should be very grateful if you could manage to call tomorrow.

I remain,
Yours most sincerely,
Gytha

* * *

Her hand-writing, Lord Locke noticed, was very elegant.

The letter, he thought, was well phrased.

He put it into his pocket, then returned to entertaining his guests.

They enjoyed an excellent luncheon.

Afterwards Lucy Compton and the gentleman with whom she was enamoured begged to stay another night.

They would return to London early the next morning.

"We are so comfortable here, dearest Valiant," Lucy Compton said, "and it will be such fun to be alone with you and Perry without your turbulent Princess who casts an evil spell on me every time I talk to you."

Lord Locke laughed a little ruefully.

"She really does make me feel frightened!" Lucy went on. "So, as we are such old friends, let us enjoy ourselves."

As Lady Compton was very witty besides being beautiful, the evening passed very pleasantly.

Only when they went up to bed did Lord Locke realise it had been an evening of wisecracks and laughter.

It was then that he suddenly began to feel guilty about Gytha.

"I suppose," he told himself, "I ought to have written to her and perhaps sent some flowers."

He made a note in his mind.

The following day when he called at Sullivan Hall he would take her some orchids.

He had noticed they were just coming into bloom in the hot-houses.

"When are you going back to London?" Perry asked when they were saying goodnight.

"As soon as I can tidy up the mess here," Lord Locke

answered. "I cannot leave that poor child to the mercy of her despicable cousins."

"No, of course not," Perry agreed, "and if there is anything I can do to help, you know I am only too willing. I had a great admiration for her father: in fact, he was one of the nicest men I have ever met."

"I feel the same," Lord Locke agreed.

He went to sleep comfortably in his own bed without giving a thought to Zuleika and her threats.

He awoke in the morning to find that the curtains had been drawn back.

Walters was calling him at seven o'clock as he had told him to do.

As he came to full wakefulness Walters said:

"I thought you'd like to know, M'Lord, that Sir Robert Sullivan passed away last night."

Lord Locke sat up in bed.

"He is dead? How do you know this?"

"A lad from the village, M'Lord, told us the news this morning."

"I must go over after breakfast to see if there is anything I can do," Lord Locke said.

He thought as he spoke that at least Gytha's cousins would be there to make the arrangements for the Funeral.

They could help her to notify the other Sullivan relations.

He told Perry what had happened.

He said he would call on Gytha and suggest she come to stay at Locke Hall.

At least until suitable arrangements could be made for someone to be with her in the house.

"I will send a note to my Aunt who is living in the Dower House," Lord Locke said. "She is rather a bore, but a kind woman. I know she will be only too delighted to come to stay here, or alternatively to have Gytha there with her."

"That sounds a better idea," Perry said, "and then we can go back to London. Do not forget you promised the Prince Regent to attend his party next Wednesday."

"He will certainly be annoyed if I let him down," Lord Locke replied.

He and Perry rode for quite a long way before breakfast.

It was getting on to ten o'clock when Lord Locke finally set off across the Park to see Gytha.

He decided to ride through the much-disputed Monk's Wood.

It would bring him more quickly onto the Sullivan estate.

The path was overgrown, which meant he had to ride more slowly than he had intended.

He was still trotting when he noticed that a burr from one of the trees had attached itself to the right flank of his horse.

He bent forward to brush it off and in doing so saved his life.

At that very moment there was the crack of a shotgun.

A bullet passed through his top-hat, blowing it from his head and his horse reared.

Lord Locke had been in many situations of great danger in the past.

He was aware that the best thing he could do was to get away as quickly as possible.

Otherwise his assailant might take another shot at him.

He therefore bent low on his horse's back and

spurred him quickly down the ride.

In a few seconds they were out onto open ground.

Then he galloped as fast as it was possible towards Sullivan Hall.

As he went bare-headed he could hardly believe that in the quiet of the country such an attempt had been made on his life.

He knew he was not exaggerating in believing that if he had not bent forward at that particular moment, the bullet would have entered his head.

He would at this moment be lying dead in the wood.

It seemed incredible that the Sullivan brothers would dare to commit such a crime.

But he could not think of anybody else who stood to gain anything by his death.

Lord Locke was not so much shocked by what had happened.

He was extremely angry.

Those who had served under him would have known this by the squareness of his chin.

The tightness of his lips, and the hard expression in his eyes would have told them he would not treat such an assault lightly.

He rode up to the front door of Sullivan Hall.

He was determined that somebody sooner or later would pay for such a dastardly action.

He handed his gloves and whip to a footman who he thought looked somewhat scared.

He attributed this to his Master's death.

That the blinds were lowered made the house look even more gloomy and oppressive than usual.

"Where is Miss Gytha?" he asked.

"'Er be in t' Study, M'Lord."

"I will find my own way there," Lord Locke said.

He was thinking that following her grandfather's death Gytha must not be further upset.

He would approach her gently.

Then, as he walked down the passage, he heard a shrill scream.

*   *   *

The previous day Gytha had avoided seeing her two cousins.

She had spent her time in her grandfather's room.

She asked the doctor to impress upon Vincent and Jonathan that on no account were they to disturb the old man.

To tell them that he would be upset even by their presence.

"Leave everything to me, Miss Gytha," the doctor who had known her for many years said. "As I warned you, your grandfather cannot live long. The only person for whom he has any affection is yourself."

"He often has a strange way of showing it!" Gytha said in a whisper.

"I know that, my dear," the doctor replied. "At the same time he has never really got over your father's death."

Gytha went to her grandfather's bedside.

She realised how sad it was for him that he had lost his only son.

His anger and disagreeableness could all be attributed to the fact that he was railing against fate.

It had left him alive while a younger man died.

When it was bedtime, Dobson told her she should go to bed to rest.

"I'll be keepin' a watch on the Master," he said.

"You will call me if he wants me?"

"Yes, of course, Miss."

Gytha had therefore gone to bed.

She was still brushing her hair in front of the mirror, when there was a knock on her door.

"You'd better come quick, Miss," Dobson called.

Without saying anything Gytha ran along the corridor to her grandfather's room.

She saw at once that he was breathing in a strange way.

However, as she sat at his bedside and took his hand in hers, he opened his eyes.

"I am here, Grandpapa," Gytha said, feeling that he did not recognise her.

For a moment she thought his fingers tightened on hers.

Then in a voice she could hardly hear he murmured:

"Alex's—daughter."

"Yes, that is right. I am Gytha."

He shut his eyes.

She thought he had gone to sleep, but was still breathing heavily.

Then his lips moved and she could just hear him.

"My—heir!" he murmured.

Then he died.

It was Dobson who took her from the bedroom.

Dobson who sent for the doctor.

Dobson who told Vincent and Jonathan what had happened.

She had lain awake a long time.

She knew with a sinking of her heart that now she would have to cope with Vincent and Jonathan ranting at her over her grandfather's money.

She was afraid, even though she knew Lord Locke was there to protect her.

In the morning, however, she knew there were a great many things to do.

Many people to notify, and she made a tremendous effort.

She put on a white muslin gown with a black sash and went downstairs.

To her relief there was no sign of either of the brothers.

When she asked rather nervously where they were, she was told they had gone out.

"I thinks, Miss," the footman said who had answered her question, "Mr. Vincent were a-goin' shootin'."

"Going shooting?" Gytha questioned in surprise.

"'E took a rifle wi' 'im, Miss."

Gytha thought this rather strange.

She could not imagine why he would want such a rifle if he was shooting pigeons or rabbits.

Then she gave a little exclamation of horror!

Perhaps he was shooting the stags in the Park.

Because she had been so much alone and so few visitors had come to the house, the stags had in the past year become tame.

They would eat from her hand.

They seldom ran away unless they were chased by a dog.

Her grandfather, at her request, had given strict instructions to the game-keepers that the stags were not to be shot.

There were, in fact, far more of them than there should be.

But Gytha loved to see them resting in the shadows of the trees.

"I cannot believe that Vincent would do anything so cruel as to kill one of them!" she reassured herself.

But she could not think of any other reason why he should take a rifle from the Gun-Room.

She went to her grandfather's Study.

She began to make a list of all the relations to whom she must write and inform them of his death.

She knew that the doctor would come later in the morning with the undertaker.

Everything appertaining to the Funeral could be left in their hands.

"I certainly must not offend anybody by leaving them out," she told herself.

She started a letter to an aged relation who lived in Bath who was very unlikely to travel so far for the Funeral.

Emily, the maid who looked after her, came into the room.

"I forgets to tell you, Miss," she said, "as it slipped me mind, that a wedding-present arrived for you last night."

"A wedding-present?" Gytha exclaimed.

"Yes, Miss, an' it seemed so strange that it should come just when the Master was a-dyin', so to speak, that I forgets about it 'til now."

"How do you know it is a wedding-present?" Gytha asked.

She was looking at what appeared to be a round basket in Emily's arms.

"A man bring it to the door, Miss. 'Twere quite late, after you'd gone to bed. He says he's lost his way, but he's brought you a wedding-present."

Gytha stared at Emily in astonishment and then thought:

'If it really is a wedding-present, it will have to be sent back when the engagement comes to an end.'

This was something she had never anticipated.

She could not imagine who would send her a wedding-present.

Her engagement to Lord Locke was still a secret except to Perry and the Princess Zuleika.

Then it struck her that it might be a present from Lord Locke.

It was just the sort of kind thing he would do to try to cheer her up for not being able to dine at the Hall.

"Let us see what it is, Emily," she said. "Open it while I finish this letter."

Emily put the basket down on the floor.

She began to untie the strings as Gytha continued:

> . . . and I do hope, Cousin Bertha, that you will be able to come to Grandpapa's Funeral, and that we shall meet again.
>
> I remain,
> Your affectionate Cousin,
> Gytha

As she signed her name Emily opened the basket.

Then she gave a scream of horror.

"Miss—Gytha! Miss—Gytha!" she exclaimed.

Gytha looked up.

The basket was open, the lid lying back.

She could see curled up in the centre of it something alive and dark.

Then as she stared Emily gave another scream.

Scrambling up in an armchair, she stood trembling, holding her skirts round her.

It was a snake, which Gytha recognised as a large poisonous adder.

It slid from the basket onto the carpet.

It moved hissing towards the desk at which Gytha was sitting.

She got up and as quickly as Emily had done, climbed first onto a chair, then onto the desk itself.

"It's poisonous! It'll kill us! Oh, Miss Gytha, what're we to do?"

As she spoke the snake turned towards her and she screamed.

Then as she screamed again, the door opened and Lord Locke stood there.

It took him only a second to assess the situation.

"Stay where you are," he said sharply, "and do not make a noise!"

Gytha heard him running back towards the Hall.

The snake moving relentlessly over the thick carpet as if in search of its prey turned back towards Gytha.

She knew she was safe.

At the same time the whole thing was unexpected and terrifying.

She could only thank God that Lord Locke was there.

She was saying a little prayer of thankfulness when she heard him returning.

She knew before she saw what he held in his hand what he was about to do.

She had expected him to be carrying a shot-gun.

Instead, he held one of her father's duelling-pistols.

Then a shot rang out, seeming unnaturally loud being confined by four walls.

The adder was dead though its tail continued to twitch.

It was then that Emily burst into tears.

"It is all right," Lord Locke said soothingly. "It is all over. It cannot hurt you now."

Quickly the maid climbed down from the chair.

Bawling like a frightened child, she rushed from the room.

Lord Locke picked the adder up by the tail, dropped it into the basket, and closed the lid.

Then he went to Gytha and lifted her down onto the floor.

"How in God's name did that get there?" he asked.

For a moment she leant against him as if for support.

He saw that she was very pale.

"It . . . it was sent to . . . me as a . . . wedding-present."

"By whom?"

"I have no idea . . . it came last night . . . and Emily forgot about it . . . until just now . . . The person who . . . left it at the door . . . gave no name."

Lord Locke's lips tightened.

"I want you to come to stay at Locke Hall," he said, "until you can make arrangements for one of your relatives to be with you. I have already sent a letter to my Aunt who lives in the Dower House to ask her to chaperon you."

Gytha looked up at him.

He thought she looked like a child who was waiting to be told what to do.

She was quite incapable of looking after herself.

He put his arm around her shoulders and said:

"Leave everything to me. Just tell your maid when she recovers from her shock to pack what you need and it will be collected later. I have already ordered my Phaeton to meet me here and I can drive you home in it."

"May I really . . . come with . . . you?" Gytha asked.

"I am going to insist on it!" Lord Locke replied. "I

do not consider your cousins are suitable companions for you at this moment. . . ."

He paused and wondered if he should say what was in his mind.

Then he decided it would be a mistake to keep to himself what had happened.

". . . especially," he continued, "as one of them has just attempted to kill me!"

"It . . . cannot be true!"

"Somebody took a pot-shot at me when I was coming through the ride in Monk's Wood."

"I cannot believe it," Gytha gasped.

"If I had not happened to bend forward at that precise moment," Lord Locke went on, "it would have entered my head, and I should not have reached you."

Gytha gave a cry of horror. Then she said:

"It was Vincent! I wondered why he had taken . . . a rifle with him. I was . . . afraid he was going to . . . kill one of the . . . stags."

"Instead, he was going to kill me!" Lord Locke said. "No doubt it was in an effort to be rid of me. We will have to be careful, you and I, Gytha."

Gytha looked up at him, and said in a small voice:

"And I think it . . . must have been the . . . Princess who . . . sent me the snake."

"Why should you think that?" Lord Locke asked.

It was what he thought himself.

But he wanted to know Gytha's reasons for suspecting it.

"She told me that you . . . belonged to . . . her and that . . . if I tried to . . . come between you and her . . . I would be sorry . . . very sorry for my . . . presumption."

As she spoke, Gytha could still hear the threatening note in the Princess's voice.

She remembered how frightened she had been.

Yet it seemed inconceivable that anything so terrifying as a poisonous adder could have been sent to her by another woman.

Instinctively she drew closer to Lord Locke as if she needed his protection.

"What are we to do?" she asked. "How can we escape if three . . . people . . . Vincent and Jonathan and the . . . Princess . . . are determined we shall . . . die."

"If I have to die," Lord Locke replied, "it will not be by a bullet fired at me by a man who is too much of a coward to face me!"

"But . . . you cannot . . . always be on your . . . guard."

Lord Locke knew this was true.

But because he did not want Gytha upset he said:

"What we are going to do now is to run away from all this unpleasantness. I am sure your father would have agreed that a good General always knows when it is wise to retreat!"

He knew as he spoke he had said the right thing in reminding Gytha of her father.

After a moment she said:

"I am sure it is Papa who told me to . . . come to . . . you for help when I was so afraid that Grandpapa would make me . . . marry one of my cousins. But he would not have . . . wished me to put . . . your life in . . . danger."

"He certainly would not want you killed by anything so unpleasant as an adder," Lord Locke said. "Now we have to be sensible enough to work out exactly who our enemies are, and how we can make sure of defeating them."

His arms tightened and he hugged her as a brother might have done as he said:

"Hurry up now, and get some clothes together. Then I will take you to my house so that we can sort this out in comfort, without feeling there are scorpions hidden in the chairs and guns pointing at us from the chandeliers."

He spoke so lightly that Gytha found herself giving a nervous little laugh.

She moved from the shelter of his arms towards the door.

Only as she reached it did she look back to say:

"I am . . . ashamed and . . . horrified that all this should have happened because I asked you to . . . help me. At the same time . . . I am thanking God . . . and Papa in my heart . . . because you are . . . h-here."

There were tears in her eyes as she said the last words.

Lord Locke heard her running down the passage.

Then he looked at the basket on the floor containing the dead adder.

He could hardly credit that such things were happening in the peace and quiet of England.

chapter six

LORD Locke was waiting impatiently in the Hall as Gytha came downstairs.

The Phaeton had arrived.

He sent a groom back with his horse with orders for a carriage to come later and fetch her luggage.

Gytha hurried down, wearing a black fur-trimmed cape which had belonged to her mother.

She also wore a bonnet from which she had quickly taken the blue ribbons and replaced them with black.

She was aware that she had been keeping Lord Locke waiting.

But when she reached his side she said:

"Please . . . I must speak to . . . you."

"We can talk as we drive," he replied.

She knew he was eager to get away.

He was anticipating there might be a nasty scene if Vincent returned and he accused him of shooting at him in the wood.

"Please," Gytha pleaded.

Without arguing, he followed her to the door of the Morning-Room.

It was nearest to where they were standing.

As she shut the door behind them Gytha said:

"There is . . . something I must . . . say."

"What is it?" Lord Locke enquired.

"I . . . I asked you to help me, and you have been very . . . very kind and . . . understanding. But I never dreamt for . . . one moment that it would mean putting your life in . . . danger."

She took a deep breath, then she went on:

"That is why I suggest that I stay . . . here and . . . help my Cousins."

Lord Locke stared at her questioningly to see if she was sincere in what she was asking.

He could not imagine that any other woman of his acquaintance would not cling to him for protection.

She would also whine about how frightened she was.

"If I do as you ask," he said slowly after a moment, "how will you manage?"

"I have thought . . . about that," Gytha replied. "I know if I offer Vincent and Jonathan . . . all the money Grandpapa has . . . left me . . . and the house, they will be . . . content without my having to . . . marry either of them."

She did not look at Lord Locke as she spoke.

He was, however, aware that her eyes would be dark with fear.

He was near enough to realise, too, that she was trembling.

"And what then will happen to you?" he asked quietly.

"Perhaps I could keep . . . just enough . . . money to have a . . . cottage somewhere on the estate . . . and Vincent might let me look after . . . the horses as I am . . . doing now. I will be . . . quite all . . . right."

"And do you really think that if your father were in the same position as I am, he would agree to that?"

He knew as he spoke that he had said the right thing.

122

Gytha looked at him and he saw the light of hope in her eyes.

"You . . . really mean," she said hesitatingly, "that you would risk going on . . . helping me as you have been . . . doing?"

"It is what I definitely intend to do," Lord Locke said. "You and I are going to face the danger together, knowing where it comes from."

She put out her hand as if she would touch him.

Then she changed her mind and said in a voice which she strove to control:

"I . . . I had to give you a . . . chance . . . to leave me. It is . . . not really your . . . fight."

"As I very much dislike people taking pot-shots at me, it is now!"

Then in a different tone of voice he added:

"Come along! We are wasting time and the sooner we find ourselves in the safety of Locke Hall the better. At the same time, I am very grateful to you for thinking of me."

She looked at him again.

Now he saw an expression in her eyes which made him uneasy.

"If the child falls in love with me," he told himself, "it will make things more complicated than they are already."

Almost brusquely he walked to the door and opened it, saying:

"We are wasting time and I am quite certain the horses are getting restless, which is definitely something to be avoided."

The way he spoke made Gytha give a little choked laugh.

Then they were outside.

He helped her into his Phaeton.

As they drove away, Gytha felt as if he carried her up into the sky on wings and everything that was frightening and unpleasant were left behind.

They sped along the dusty lanes.

It made the distance to Locke Hall far longer than if they had gone back the way Lord Locke had come.

They did not speak.

Gytha was murmuring a prayer of thanks.

She was leaving Vincent and Jonathan behind in the dark house, with her grandfather lying dead in his bedroom.

He had been laid out before she saw him again.

She thought he looked very dignified in death.

The expression on his face was far kinder than it had been when he was alive.

She said a prayer beside him.

Then Dobson had hurried her from the room, saying:

"It's no use you upsettin' yourself, Miss Gytha. Th' Master's at peace an' he'll not suffer any more pain."

Now Lord Locke had taken charge.

She would have to go back for the Funeral.

But she felt as if the darkness that encompassed her had been swept away.

She had suddenly come into the sunlight.

"Thank you . . . God . . . for letting him . . . protect me," she said in her heart.

She looked at his handsome profile etched against the sky.

His eyes were on his horses but she felt a glowing warmth seep through her.

She knew that everything had changed because he was so kind to her.

She wanted to tell him how much it meant to her.

Almost as if he were aware of her feelings, he looked down and smiled at her.

At that moment she knew she loved him.

Of course she loved him!

She had loved him since she had first seen him out hunting.

She had thought then he was the most fascinating and attractive man she had ever imagined!

Whenever she had seen him ride in a Steeple-chase he had seemed like a Knight in armour.

He was part of the Fairy Stories and Annals of Chivalry her mother had read to her when she was a child.

She must have been only fifteen when he first began to be part of her dreams.

She had encouraged the grooms to tell her about his horses.

Then he had been away for a long time, first in the Army of Occupation and then travelling round the world.

But she had talked about him to the servants.

They had relatives in the village, working at Locke Hall, and at Locke House in London.

They always had something to relate about the man whom everybody in the neighbourhood admired.

His gallantry in the war lost nothing in the telling.

The parties he gave in London on his return at which the chief guest was always the Prince Regent were described a dozen times.

Of course Gytha heard about the beautiful ladies with whom he spent his time.

She was not surprised that they invariably lost their hearts to him.

Almost every day there was something new to be exclaimed over in the village shop.

This was owned by the father of a housemaid at the Hall and of one of Lord Locke's footmen in London.

Another villager was related to His Lordship's Valet.

Gytha heard everything about the party that Lord Locke intended to give at the Hall almost before the servants in the great house were aware of it.

Now she knew the reason she had been so interested.

It was that he was the hero of all her fantasies; the man she admired above all others.

But because of the feud between their two families she thought despairingly she would never meet him.

Now she was with him, beside him, and he had promised to protect and look after her.

She thought no woman in the whole world could be so lucky.

"I love him! I love him!" she said to the rattle of the wheels and the clip-clop of the horses' hoofs.

Then she told herself she must be very careful.

He must never be aware of her feelings.

Perry was waiting for them on the steps.

As he helped Gytha down from the Phaeton he said:

"Why is Valiant driving without a hat? Was it blown off in the wind?"

"Blown off is the right word for it," Lord Locke said before Gytha could reply, "but it was not the wind that was responsible, but a bullet!"

Perry stared at him and he said:

"I will tell you about it when we are alone."

They walked into the Hall.

Gytha felt it was filled with sunshine as if in a strange way she had come home.

Lord Locke led the way into the Library.

Going to the grog-table, he poured out glasses of champagne for Gytha and himself.

He said to Perry as he did so:

"We deserve this! When I tell you what we have been through you will not believe it!"

"What on earth has happened?" Perry enquired.

"My hat was shot from my head by a bullet in the much-contested Monk's Wood," Lord Locke replied, "and Gytha was sent as a wedding-present, a poisonous adder!"

"I certainly do *not* believe it!" Perry ejaculated.

Then they both had to tell him in detail exactly what had occurred.

"It was Vincent who shot at me," Lord Locke said, "and the adder was undoubtedly Zuleika's Oriental idea of an appropriate wedding-present!"

"What do you intend to do about them?" Perry enquired again.

Lord Locke shrugged his shoulders.

"What can I do? I know they were the culprits, but my suspicions would not be accepted as evidence in a Court of Law."

"You can hardly sit down and wait for them to try again!" Perry exclaimed.

"Will you suggest then what we can do," Lord Locke asked, "short of leaving the country?"

Gytha put down her glass of champagne on a table beside her chair.

Clasping her hands together, she said:

"Please, Major Westington, listen to me! I want you to persuade His Lordship that the only sensible thing to do is for me to give the money Grandpapa has left me to my cousins. Then they will no longer have any motive to . . . kill him and he will be . . . safe."

"I will not surrender to brute force!" Lord Locke said firmly.

"No, of course not," Perry agreed, "and when it comes to a fight, Gytha, I would back Valiant against any assailant. He is the best shot with a pistol I have ever known!"

Gytha did not argue.

She thought despairingly that Vincent would never attack Lord Locke openly.

Instead, he would do what he had done already— shoot at him in a wood where he would not be seen.

He would wait until it was dark to shoot him as he was getting into a carriage.

He would wait until he was riding back from hunting.

Then he would escape before anyone could identify him.

"What can I do to save him?" she asked herself.

She felt her love for him surge up into her breast.

She wanted to tell him that she was willing to die herself rather than that he should be killed or injured on her behalf.

She did not speak.

Her frightened eyes reminded Lord Locke of a nervous fawn. Then he said:

"It is no use worrying ourselves unduly. What we have to do is to decide quite quietly and without panic how we should tackle this situation.

He smiled.

"What we need first is a good luncheon. My Nanny always told me that things would seem better on a full stomach!"

Gytha laughed as he intended she should.

Lord Locke arranged for her to be taken upstairs to where the Housekeeper was waiting.

She showed Gytha into a large bedroom that was far more beautiful than any room she had seen before.

As she took off her bonnet she said:

"My clothes are following me, but I feel rather embarrassed as I have only one black gown which belonged to my mother, and I do not think I shall have an opportunity of buying any more."

Mrs. Meadows the Housekeeper looked at her reflectively. Then she said:

"I thinks, Miss, if you're not too proud, I could fit you up until you've time to go to London, or wherever else you'll be shopping."

"You could?" Gytha asked. "But how?"

"His Lordship's sister, Miss, is at the moment in India, with her husband."

Gytha listened excitedly as Mrs. Meadows went on:

"She left over a year ago, and gave me all her winter clothes to care for, saying they would be no use to her in the heat."

"You do not think she would mind my borrowing them?" Gytha asked.

"No, of course not, Miss. In any case, I'm certain that by the time Her Ladyship returns she'll want everything she possesses replaced as being out of fashion."

"It sounds very extravagant!" Gytha murmured.

Mrs. Meadows smiled.

"Her Ladyship's husband, Sir Murrey Weldon, is a very rich gentleman, and he never denies Her Ladyship anything she needs."

Gytha had of course heard of Lord Locke's elder sister and how attractive she was.

In fact, she had been the toast of St. James's.

Three years ago she married the dashing Colonel of

the Queen's Dragoon Guards.

When Gytha heard that he had been sent out to India she had been interested.

Mostly because she had read of her grandfather's travels in that country.

She wished she, too, could be fortunate enough to visit anywhere so exciting.

Now she would have the chance of borrowing some of Lady Weldon's clothes.

She would therefore not feel as ashamed of her appearance in front of Lord Locke as she had the other night.

Then she had been aware that women like the Princess Zuleika had looked scornfully at her homemade muslin gown.

"Thank you," she said to Mrs. Meadows, "you are very kind."

"What I was thinking, Miss," Mrs. Meadows said, "is there's no need for you to wear pitch black, so to speak, when you're here alone with His Lordship and Major Westington."

She paused to see Gytha's reaction to this, and went on:

"I know Her Ladyship had some pretty mauve gowns which are half-mourning, and I thinks they'd suit you with your fair hair and white skin. In fact, if I may so, Miss, you'd look like a violet in them."

Gytha was thrilled at the idea.

Mrs. Meadows brought her one of the mauve gowns to change into for luncheon.

It was very fashionable and made of a material that was far more expensive than anything Gytha had ever bought for herself.

She therefore went downstairs feeling a little self-conscious.

She also hoped Lord Locke would think her now more suitably gowned for the grandeur of his house.

Actually it was Perry who exclaimed the moment she appeared:

"You look like a flower and far too lovely for such a small audience as Valiant and myself!"

Gytha blushed.

"'Fine feathers make fine birds,'" she said shyly, "but I am afraid in this case the feathers are... borrowed."

In case she had done something wrong, she turned to Lord Locke and said quickly:

"As my lady's-maid has not yet arrived with my own gowns... and as the one I was... wearing looked creased, Mrs. Meadows... persuaded me that... your sister would not mind if I borrowed... something of ... hers."

"No, of course she would not mind," Lord Locke replied, "and, as Perry said, you look very lovely."

He spoke in a dry voice which did not make her feel embarrassed by the compliment.

At the same time, her heart seemed to turn over in her breast.

The whole room seemed bathed in light because he was so kind to her.

She was not aware that before she joined them Perry had said to Lord Locke:

"It is a pretty serious state of affairs, Valiant. What are you going to do about it?"

"What can I do?" Lord Locke enquired.

"It is appalling behaviour on the part of Zuleika,"

Perry said, "and I would like to see you teach Sullivan a lesson for his behaviour!"

"I would like to do that myself," Lord Locke agreed, "but I am not certain how I can challenge him with an action he will obviously deny."

"You realise that unless you do something about it you will be a sitting target?"

"Of course I realise that," Lord Locke replied, "but you must not say too much and frighten Gytha."

Perry did as he was asked.

It was he who started at luncheon to make the conversation amusing and light.

There was no reference whatsoever to the drama that had taken place that morning.

Lord Locke joined in.

Gytha found herself laughing helplessly at the things the two men said.

They also argued jokingly between themselves.

They were so witty that when the meal finished Gytha thought she had never had such a happy time.

She felt nevertheless that it was somehow wrong to be happy when her grandfather had just died.

But to have got away from the dark, menacing house and her Cousins was an inexpressible relief.

She wanted to laugh and sing at the sheer joy of being free of them.

After lunch they went to the stables.

As Lord Locke had guessed, nothing could have taken her mind off what had occurred more than to inspect his horses.

There were over forty of them, and they visited each one in their stalls.

The grooms proudly brought out the finest to parade them up and down the yard.

Gytha could see the way they moved and the Arab strain in many of them.

But the men were surprised at how much she knew about horses and the process of breeding.

She also told the Head Groom of a new poultice that she had made from herbs and which had proved most effective.

He promised to try it should occasion arise.

Time passed very quickly.

She could hardly believe it possible when Lord Locke said it was long past teatime and he was sure it would be waiting for them in the house.

*　　*　　*

Only after tea was over and Gytha went upstairs on Lord Locke's suggestion to lie down before dinner did she find herself wondering what was happening at home.

When she left she had asked Emily to tell her Cousins when they returned that she had gone to stay at Locke Hall.

"Mr. Vincent said he'd be back for luncheon," Emily replied, "but I thinks Mr. Jonathan's gone to London."

"To London?" Gytha exclaimed in surprise. "Then he will not be returning tonight."

"He said he might be late but he was definitely acoming back."

Gytha wondered why he should have gone to London.

Then it struck her that he had probably gone to consult a Lawyer.

They would want to know how they could contest the Will.

The thought made her all the more eager to get away.

At the same time, she had known it was only right that she should offer Lord Locke the chance to be free of her.

She lay on the bed in the beautiful bedroom wearing a silk *negligée* trimmed with lace which had belonged to Lord Locke's sister.

She felt as if she had stepped into a story-book and become unexpectedly a Fairy Princess.

Never had she imagined herself in such glamorous and lovely surroundings.

Later, she had a bath scented with honeysuckle.

Mrs. Meadows then brought her two evening-gowns from which she could choose.

One was made in a very soft pale mauve, much the same colour as she had worn at luncheon.

The other was white and simply but exquisitely made in white chiffon.

Because it was so lovely Gytha hesitated.

She knew it did not look like mourning.

Then she was lost.

"Can I really wear it?" she asked Mrs. Meadows eagerly.

"Of course you can, Miss, and very beautiful you'll look in it, if I may say so."

"Are you quite certain Her Ladyship will not mind?"

"Mind? She says to me last time she wore that gown that she was sick of it and I were not to bring it out for her again!"

As she put it on, Gytha saw how it gave her an elegant figure she never knew she possessed.

She found it difficult to believe that any woman could be tired of a gown that was so lovely.

It was also very obviously the work of an expensive Court Dressmaker.

Mrs. Meadows helped her to arrange her hair in a more fashionable mode.

Then she fixed two white camelias on either side of her head.

She then arranged several more at the point of her *décolletage*.

Gytha looked in the mirror.

She thought she had never looked like this before in the whole of her life.

She remembered how Lord Locke had said this morning that she was lovely.

She hoped that he would say the same this evening.

Having thanked Mrs. Meadows for her kindness, she began to walk down the stairs.

She felt she was still the Fairy-tale Princess she had thought herself to be in her bedroom.

She had reached the bottom of the stairs, when the footman who was on duty said:

"'Scuse me, Miss, but there's an old lady outside in a carriage asking if you'd be kind enough t' go out an' speak to her as she's come special t' see you, but isn't well enough to come into th' house."

"An old lady?" Gytha queried. "I wonder who it could be?"

"She didn't give 'er name, Miss, but she says as 'twas important for her t' speak t' you."

It flashed through Gytha's mind that it might be something concerning the servants in the Sullivan household.

"Of course I will speak to her," she said to the footman.

"'Tis cold out there, Miss," he said. "If you'll wait a minute, I'll fetch you somethin' to put on."

He went to a large, carved wardrobe that stood in one

corner of the Hall, and pulled out a fur cape.

He put it round Gytha's shoulders.

"Thank you," she said. "It is very kind of you to think of it."

The footman opened the front door.

She ran lightly down the steps to where a closed carriage was waiting.

The footman from the box opened the carriage-door as she reached it.

She looked in, aware in the fading light that somebody was sitting on the back-seat.

"You wanted to speak to me?" she asked.

As she spoke the footman gave her a push.

A hand came from the figure on the back-seat and pulled her forward.

As they did so the door of the carriage was shut and the horses started off.

"What . . . are you . . . doing? What is . . . happening?" Gytha cried.

Then the presumed old lady pulled away a black shawl and she saw who it was.

"Cousin Vincent!" she exclaimed. "What are . . . you doing? How . . . dare you . . . take me away . . . like this!"

As she spoke, Jonathan, who had been sitting on the floor, pushed off the rug which covered him.

He rose to sit on the seat with his back to the horses.

She looked at him in astonishment.

She could see that he was grinning as he said in his usual unpleasantly silky manner:

"Dear little Gytha! How nice to see you again!"

"You have no right to behave . . . like this!" Gytha cried angrily.

"I think we have every right," Vincent contradicted.

"You sneaked out of the house when we were both away. How could you do anything so disgraceful with your poor grandfather not yet in his grave?"

Gytha steadied herself on the back-seat.

She sat as far away from her Cousin Vincent as it was possible.

She realised in horror that she was being taken by force away from Lord Locke.

"As you left in such a hurry without saying goodbye to us," Vincent said in his slow, sarcastic drawl, "Jonathan and I have decided that there shall be no more arguments about your future."

"What do . . . you . . . mean?" Gytha asked.

"We are going now to the Church," he answered, "where I, as the oldest member and in fact the head of the family, will marry you."

For a moment Gytha thought she could not have heard him aright.

Then she said furiously:

"How dare you behave in this outrageous fashion. If you think I will marry you, then you are very much . . . mistaken!"

"You have no choice, my dear Gytha," Vincent said, unpleasantly. "I have a loaded pistol in my pocket, and if you try to disobey me, I shall not hesitate to injure you so that you will find it difficult to escape a second time."

He paused a moment to snarl at her.

"A bullet in your leg will cripple you for at least a month."

Because Gytha was so angry, without thinking she retorted:

"Perhaps you will miss me, as you missed Lord Locke this morning!"

"So you knew it was I who shot at him?" Vincent sneered. "Well, there will be no need for me to kill him once you are my wife."

"There is no need for you to marry me," Gytha said. "As I have already told Lord Locke, I intend to let you and Jonathan have my money and the house so long as you leave His Lordship and me alone."

"A very commendable idea," Vincent said mockingly, "but I expect in that case there would be a great deal of trouble from the Trustees of Uncle Robert's estate."

His voice was even more unpleasant as he finished:

"Whereas, if you are my wife, there will be no difficulty."

"I will not . . . marry you . . . I absolutely . . . refuse!" Gytha cried.

"Then I will carry out my threat, which is not an idle one," Vincent said. "And I am quite certain that even if you are a little dazed with pain, that you will be capable of repeating your marriage vows."

She did not speak, and Vincent said:

"Of course, if you make no difficulties and do as I say, I am prepared to give you my word that I will no longer attack or threaten Lord Locke in any way."

He laughed, and it was an ugly sound, before he added:

"I imagine, like so many other foolish women, you have lost your heart to him, therefore it might be a comfort for you to know that as far as I am concerned, he will no longer be in any danger."

Gytha drew in her breath.

She realised that Vincent was more perceptive than she had expected.

He was aware, in his own crafty way, that she was in love with Lord Locke.

He guessed, too, that to save him she would be willing to sacrifice herself.

She made one last bid for freedom.

"If you and Jonathan will take my money," she said, "I am sure it can be quite easily arranged. All I would ask would be a small cottage for myself on the estate, and perhaps a field where I can keep the horses."

"It is too late," Vincent replied.

His eyes roamed over her insultingly as he said:

"I have already said, I have made up my mind that you will suit me admirably as a wife, and Jonathan has been kind enough to obtain a Special Licence so that there should be no difficulties—unless you make them."

"They have thought of everything," Gytha told herself despairingly.

Then as she knew she was trapped she began to pray.

To her father she prayed and also to Lord Locke.

She was saying over and over again as the carriage rolled on:

"Save me! Save me!"

*　　*　　*

Lord Locke came downstairs only a few seconds after Gytha had left.

Seeing the footman standing at the open front door he said sharply:

"It is very cold! Why have you got the door open?"

"I thought Miss Sullivan would be coming back, Sir."

"Miss Sullivan?"

As he spoke Bates came hurrying into the Hall with another footman behind him.

"I'm sorry, M'Lord," Bates said. "I was kept . . ."

Lord Locke, however, was not listening.

"Do you mean to say that Miss Sullivan has gone out?" he asked the footman who was closing the door.

"Yes, M'Lord. A carriage comes wi' an old lady in it as says 'er wants to speak t' Miss Sullivan, an' when she goes down to th' carriage the footman who opens th' door pushed her in! I sees it wi' me own eyes!"

"What are you talking about?" Lord Locke asked in perplexity. "I cannot understand."

Bates was now beside him and said sharply:

"Speak up, lad, tell His Lordship exactly what happened."

"It's like this," the footman said. "I tells Miss Sullivan an old lady wants t' speak t' her who's not well enough t' get out o' her carriage, so Miss Sullivan says she'll go to 'er."

He realised Lord Locke and Bates were staring at him.

"I gives 'er a fur wrap, M'Lord," he added defensively, "in case 'er were cold. . . ."

"Yes, yes," Lord Locke said. "Then what happened?"

"Like I says, M'Lord, Miss Sullivan looks into the carriage an' th' footman as opens th's door pushes her in, slams it, an' th' carriage drives off! I couldn't believe 'twere ahappening!"

Lord Locke considered this for a moment, then he asked:

"Have you ever seen the carriage or any of the people from it before?"

"No, My Lord."

There was silence. Then the footman said tentatively:

"I did 'ave an idea, M'Lord, that as they was drivin' off, I sees Mr. Jonathan Sullivan thro' th' window."

Lord Locke turned to Bates.

"Send somebody over to the stables for two horses to be saddled immediately and brought to the front door, and be quick about it!"

"Very good, M'Lord!"

Bates repeated the order to the footman standing behind him.

Lord Locke walked quickly across the hall to the Salon.

As he expected, Perry, who had come down earlier, was standing in front of the fire.

He had a glass of champagne in his hand.

"They have kidnapped Gytha!" Lord Locke announced.

"Kidnapped her? Who has?"

"The Sullivan brothers, of course! I imagine they will have taken her back to the Hall, and if we ride across country, we can be there before them."

Perry put down his glass.

He knew by the note in Lord Locke's voice that he was giving orders.

It was the way he had spoken when they were together in the Army, sharp and decisive.

Orders which were to be carried out at once.

He walked across the room.

"Are we to change?" he asked.

"No, there is no time for that."

Perry accepted the decision without comment.

As they went out into the Hall, Lord Locke said to Bates:

"Our evening-cloaks and order a closed carriage to

follow us to Sullivan House with four horses."

As Perry put on his cloak and hat Lord Locke walked quickly away.

Perry guessed that he was going to the Gun-Room.

He returned with a duelling-pistol in each hand.

The horses were already coming round from the stables.

Lord Locke handed one of the pistols to Perry, saying as he did so:

"It is primed."

Without comment, Perry put it into his pocket.

As soon as his cloak was over his shoulders Lord Locke did the same thing.

The two men ran down the steps and swung themselves into the saddle.

They set off at a sharp pace.

Lord Locke led the way towards Monk's Wood, which would be the quickest route.

As he watched them go, Bates ejaculated beneath his breath:

"I've never in all me born days seen such going on —never!"

chapter seven

IT was growing dark.

The two riders had to slow their pace slightly in the wood.

Lord Locke was very conscious that it was here that Vincent had fired at him.

Only by a hair's-breadth had he escaped being killed.

The mere thought of it made him more and more angry.

He vowed that when he caught up with the Sullivan brothers, he would teach them a lesson.

Then he was worrying over Gytha.

He was aware how much being carried off in such an unpleasant manner would distress her.

He felt as if he could see her large eyes dark with fear.

She pleaded with him to save her.

He knew it was something he must do and quickly.

"It is intolerable that any woman should be treated in such a brutal fashion!" he muttered beneath his breath.

Then he knew he was not thinking of just any woman but specifically of Gytha.

She was so helpless.

She was also sensitive and very easily frightened.

He remembered how she had trembled the first day she had come to the Hall to ask him for help.

How shy she had been.

It had been difficult for her to say what she wanted.

Her eyes would not meet his!

As he thought of it, he knew that shyness was something he had seldom, if ever, encountered in a woman.

It was, he thought, extremely attractive.

She was lovely when her long eye-lashes touched her pale cheeks.

When he made her blush her skin was suffused with colour like the dawn rising in the sky.

"She is beautiful!" he said to himself. "If she were taken to London and presented to the Social World, she would shine like a star."

Then he thought perhaps that might spoil her.

He wanted her to remain as she was.

Unspoilt, unselfconscious, gentle, and sweet to a degree that he had never found in any other woman.

At the same time, she had an intelligence.

Perry had appreciated it first, and he had been forced to acknowledge later.

"She is quite exceptional," he murmured.

Then he thought furiously it was no less exceptional for her to endure this sort of experience.

It was quite inconceivable for a young girl ordinarily.

Who could imagine that Gytha would be pressured by her despicable Cousins into accepting one of them as a husband.

That she would be kidnapped from his own house.

That she would be taken away in such an unseemly fashion.

"I will kill them for this!" he exclaimed through his teeth.

He quickened his pace so that Perry was pushed to keep up with him.

They reached Sullivan House to find it shrouded in darkness.

There was no light shining out of any of the windows.

Lord Locke drew his horse to a standstill under some trees opposite the front-door.

As Perry drew alongside him, he said:

"I imagine we have got here more quickly than the carriage because it is longer by road, but they should arrive any moment now."

Perry did not answer.

He was adjusting his evening-cape.

He was thinking it was extremely uncomfortable to ride in evening-clothes.

He and Lord Locke were both wearing the long drain-pipe trousers invented by the Prince Regent.

On less formal occasions they replaced the knee-breeches which had hitherto been compulsory for dinner.

"The house certainly looks gloomy," Perry said at last.

"Sir Robert has not yet been buried," Lord Locke replied.

As he spoke, he turned his head.

He was looking down the long drive.

At the far end of it was the Churchyard, where he knew Sir Robert would soon be laid to rest.

Perry also turned to look in the same direction, then he exclaimed:

"Is that the Church? If so, they must be holding a Service."

As he spoke Lord Locke saw there were lights showing through the branches of the trees.

"By God! That is where they have taken Gytha!" he exclaimed.

He spurred his horse forward as he spoke and galloped down the long drive.

He reached the lychgate of the Churchyard.

He saw, as he had expected, a closed carriage standing outside it.

The coachman was witting on the box.

There was a footman beside the horses.

Lord Locke flung himself from the saddle.

Sharply and in a tone of authority he said:

"Hold our horses!"

Then he and Perry were racing up the narrow path which led to the Church door.

*　　*　　*

The carriage containing Gytha had been travelling for nearly a mile before she spoke again.

Then she said in a low, pleading voice:

"Please . . . Cousin Vincent . . . listen to me. I am prepared to . . . give you every penny . . . I possess if I do not . . . have to . . . marry you."

"I do not intend to discuss it with you any further," Vincent answered sharply. "You will marry me, and I am not making idle threats when I say that I will wound you if you make a fuss."

He added with a sneer:

"Moreover, I will certainly make sure that your precious Lord Locke does not escape me another time."

"Perhaps dear little Gytha would rather marry me!" Jonathan chimed in.

"Shut up!" Vincent said rudely. "I have no intention of having my plans disrupted, and I have promised to

146

look after you once I have Gytha's money in my hands."

"I only hope you will keep your word," Jonathan whined.

"I consider it an insult that you should question it!" Vincent retorted.

Hearing the two brothers wrangling with each other, Gytha wanted to scream.

It was what, she thought, she would have to listen to for the rest of her life.

Inevitably the bone of contention between them would always be her money.

The idea was horrible.

She was praying again for Lord Locke.

She felt as if her whole being winged towards him.

She had, however, little hope that he could come in time to save her.

Once she was married to Vincent, there would be no escape.

She would be his wife.

No one, not even Lord Locke, could take her away from him.

"I love ... you! I love ... you!" she cried in her heart. "Save ... me! Oh, please ... save ... me!"

The horses came to a standstill.

She saw the lychgate through the carriage-window and knew her last hope had gone.

The footman got down from the box to open the door.

Jonathan stepped out first, followed by Vincent.

They walked each side of her up the path which led to the Church porch.

She felt like a prisoner being taken to the place of execution.

As they passed her mother's grave she gave one last silent cry for help.

"Help me, Mama, help me! If I have to . . . marry Vincent . . . then I must die, for I could . . . not tolerate living . . . with . . . him!"

It was a cry of desperation.

She felt she was drowning and the waters were closing over her.

Then they entered the Church, and the candles were lit on the altar.

The old Vicar who had Christened her and whom she had known all her life was waiting.

At the sight of him she thought that here was one last chance.

He was very old and rather deaf.

She knew, however, that if she pleaded with him, he would refuse to marry her to Vincent.

Instinctively Vincent guessed what was passing through her mind.

He stopped still and said in a low voice:

"If you make a scene or try to persuade the old fool not to marry us, I will shoot him as well as you. So keep your mouth shut unless you want his blood on your hands."

Gytha did not reply.

She only shut her eyes.

She felt it was impossible that any man who bore her father's name could be so utterly despicable.

Vincent put her hand through his arm.

He started to walk slowly and with what he thought was dignity up the aisle.

Jonathan followed them.

They reached the altar-steps and stopped in front of the Vicar.

He was going blind, and he peered at Gytha through his spectacles.

Then he smiled at her.

"Bless you, my child," he said. "I understand you wish to be married to your Cousin Vincent."

Gytha parted her lips to say it was the last thing she wanted.

"You have the Special Licence," Vincent said sharply. "Get on with the Service."

He spoke in a manner which would have been unpardonably rude to a servant.

It was grossly insulting to an elderly Clergyman.

The Vicar looked at Vincent reprovingly.

Gytha had a faint hope that he would refuse to marry them.

Slowly he opened his Prayer-Book and began the Marriage-Service:

"'Dearly Beloved. We are gathered together here . . .'"

"Cut all that!" Vincent ordered. "And just marry us."

"I have been performing the Marriage-Service for many years, Mr. Sullivan," the Vicar replied quietly, "and I will not alter what is set down in the Prayer-Book."

"Very well," Vincent said sullenly, "but we are in a hurry."

Deliberately slowly because he was shocked by Vincent's behaviour the Vicar began again:

"'Dearly Beloved. We are . . .'"

At that moment there was was a clatter of footsteps outside the church.

Gytha held her breath.

She heard the door which Jonathan had closed behind them open.

She knew with a leap of her heart who had come into the Church.

"Stop this marriage!"

Lord Locke's voice rang out.

It seemed to echo round the building.

Gytha turned to see him coming down the aisle.

As she did so she was aware that Vincent was pulling his pistol from his pocket.

"Be . . . careful! Be . . . careful!" she screamed. "He will . . . shoot you!"

As she spoke she flung herself against Vincent.

She tried to force the pistol that was pointing at Lord Locke up into the air.

Vincent thrust her violently away from him.

In doing so he inadvertently pulled the trigger.

With a resounding explosion a bullet seared its way into one of the pillars.

It gave Lord Locke time to reach Vincent.

With a strong upper-cut on the chin he knocked him over the communion-rail.

He fell unconscious on the other side of it.

As he did so, Jonathan gave a cry of horror.

Lord Locke turned and punched him in the same manner.

He fell backwards onto the tiled floor with a crash.

Gytha had staggered when Vincent pushed her away from him, but she had not lost her balance.

With shining eyes she threw herself against Lord Locke, crying:

"You . . . came! You . . . came! I prayed to you to . . . save me . . . but I . . . thought you would be . . . too late."

As he looked down at her they heard the old Vicar ask quaveringly:

"What is happening? This is wrong, very wrong in God's house!"

"I am sorry . . . Vicar," Gytha said a little unsteadily,

"but . . . I was being . . . forced into . . . marriage against my . . . will . . . and now Lord Locke has . . . saved me!"

"Against your will, my child?" the Vicar repeated. "Why did you not tell me so? I thought such a hasty marriage was wrong, but that it was what you wished."

"I will see to it that everything is explained to you tomorrow," Lord Locke said, "but first I must take Gytha away."

In a quiet, calm voice he went on:

"I suggest, Vicar, that you go back to the Vicarage and leave the two Sullivan brothers, who have behaved disgracefully, to recover their senses."

The Vicar looked around him in a bewildered fashion.

Lord Locke saw that lying on the side table next to the Altar there was a Special Licence.

He bent over the rail and picked it up.

He noticed as he did so that Vincent, sprawled in an undignified position on the other side of it, was still unconscious.

There was a faint smile on his lips.

He put his arm around Gytha and helped her down the aisle.

Perry having said a few further words of apology to the Vicar followed them.

By the time they had walked through the Churchyard the sky was dark.

The stars were coming out one by one.

They reached the lychgate.

As they did so they saw coming down the road the lights of Lord Locke's carriage.

It was drawn by four horses.

Lord Locke with his arm around Gytha's shoulders could feel her trembling against him.

The carriage came to a standstill and the footman jumped down from the box.

"Ride Hercules home, James," he ordered. "Major Westington will show you the way."

"Very good, M'Lord."

Lord Locke's horse and Perry's were still being held by Vincent's groom.

The man was staring at them open-mouthed.

Perry opened the door of the carriage.

Lord Locke, having lifted Gytha in, stood outside.

He spoke to Perry in a low voice.

He was giving him, Gytha was sure, instructions.

She could not hear what they were and had no wish to do so.

All she was thinking and feeling was that like the Archangel Michael, Lord Locke had saved her.

He had swept down from the Heavens at the very last moment.

She had thought despairingly that she was completely and utterly lost.

Then she heard Perry say:

"I will do what you say, Valiant, and let me add I have never seen you in better form. Gentleman Jackson would have been proud of you!"

"I am rather proud of myself," Lord Locke said with a smile.

He stepped into the carriage.

The horses turned round to drive back the way they had come.

Lord Locke put his arms around Gytha and pulled her gently against him.

"It is all over," he said quietly, "but this must never happen again."

It was then for the first time that Gytha burst into tears.

She hid her face against his shoulder.

She was crying with sheer relief because her prayers had been answered.

"You . . . saved me . . . you . . . saved me," she whispered. "I . . . I knew that . . . if I had to . . . marry Vincent . . . I would rather . . . d-die."

"It is all over," Lord Locke said again.

He touched her shoulder soothingly as he spoke and realised she was very cold.

"You must be frozen," he exclaimed.

He undid the clasp of his evening-cloak.

He drew it from his shoulders and wrapped it round her.

Then once again he pulled her close to him and she was no longer crying.

"How could . . . you have been so . . . wonderful as to come so . . . quickly?" she asked. "I thought you would not . . . understand what had . . . happened to me . . . and even if you . . . followed us . . . you would be . . . too late."

"You are not to think about it anymore."

She looked up at him.

As there was a candle-lantern alight inside the carriage he could see the fear in her eyes.

Her lips were trembling as she said:

"Vincent . . . said if I did not . . . marry him . . . he would . . . kill you."

"Did that upset you?" Lord Locke asked.

"Upset . . . me?" Gytha repeated. "How can you . . . ask such a . . . foolish question? How can I let you die? How . . . can I . . . bear it . . . if he wounded you?"

153

There was an agony in her voice.

It revealed very clearly her terror that such a thing might still happen.

"Then if you feel like that," Lord Locke said, "I have a very easy solution to offer."

"A . . . solution?"

Now the tears were once again running down her cheeks.

Lord Locke took a handkerchief from his pocket and wiped them away.

"Yes, I have a solution," he said, "but I am rather afraid to suggest it in case it is something you would dislike."

"I . . . I do not . . . understand."

He paused for a moment.

Then looking into her eyes he said:

"I think, Gytha, that if you were really worried over your Cousin killing or maiming me, that you must like me a little."

"Of course I like you!" Gytha replied. "You are so wonderful . . . so magnificent . . . and only you could have . . . saved me."

"And you like me just for that, or is there any other reason?"

Her eyes were held by him and she could not look away.

He thought nothing could be more revealing.

No woman could look at him more adoringly.

"Tell me what you feel," he asked softly.

She was then aware of what he was thinking, her eye-lashes dark against her cheeks.

With a little murmur she hid her face again.

Lord Locke's lips rested on her forehead as he said:

"I think, darling, you love me a little."

He felt her quiver, then she whispered:

"Of course I . . . love you! How could I not . . . love anybody so . . . wonderful . . . but . . . I did not want you to . . . know about it."

"I cannot help knowing since I love you too!"

For a moment Gytha was still.

Then she raised her face to look at him incredulously.

"You . . . love me?"

The words were almost inaudible.

"I love you!" he said firmly. "I have loved you for a long time, but I would not acknowledge it to myself."

His voice dropped a little as he went on:

"Then when those devils took you away, I knew that if I lost you, I would lose something so perfect, so precious, that my life would never be the same again."

Gytha gave a little cry.

"How . . . can you . . . say such . . . things to . . . me? How can you . . . think them?"

"I can think them and I can say them because I love you," Lord Locke said, "and I want to go on and on telling you of my love."

He smiled.

"So, my darling, to make it easier and to make quite sure you are safe and can never be spirited away from me again, we are going to be married tonight!"

Gytha stared at him as if she could not believe what she had heard.

"I will have to change the name of the bridegroom on the Special Licence," he continued, "which your Cousin Vincent obtained."

He smiled at her and then added:

"The Archbishop of Canterbury when he was a young man was my father's Chaplain, at Locke Hall, so I feel certain he will understand the necessity for it."

"Then . . . you can . . . marry me?" Gytha asked.

"I am going to marry you, and then there will be no more dramas with your Cousins or dubious wedding-presents that have to be exterminated."

"How . . . can you be . . . sure of . . . that?"

Gytha's voice trembled.

He knew that once again she was frightened.

He pulled her a little closer to him before he said:

"The first thing we are going to do tomorrow morning before we leave on our honeymoon is . . ."

"Honeymoon?" Gytha whispered.

". . . before we leave on our honeymoon," Lord Locke repeated, "is to send for my Solicitors. You and I will sign a deed giving your Cousins each five thousand pounds a year and a house in London for *our* lifetime."

His voice was stern as he finished:

"If *either* of us dies, the benefit to them will cease and the house will revert to my estate."

Gytha gave a little cry.

"That is brilliant . . . very . . . very clever!"

"I think that will ensure that the Sullivan brothers will be only too eager to protect rather than assassinate us."

"You . . . are so . . . wonderful!"

"As for our other enemy," Lord Locke continued, "if anything should happen to my wife, I would be in mourning for a year, and a year is a long time in any young woman's life."

Gytha understood exactly what he was implying.

Again she said:

"How can you be so . . . clever . . . so marvellous? Now I can be . . . happy and no longer . . . afraid."

"I will not allow you to be afraid," Lord Locke said,

"and I want to show you how to be happy."

As he spoke he put his fingers under her chin.

He turned her face up to his.

Then slowly, as if he savoured the moment, his lips took possession of hers.

To Gytha it was as if the sky had opened.

He swept her up towards the stars.

He kissed her, at first gently and very tenderly, then more possessively.

She knew that this was the love she had always longed to find.

Incredibly, the hero of all her dreams was kissing her.

She was his, completely his, as she had always wanted to be.

"I . . . love you! I love . . . you!" she murmured.

His arms tightened as he added:

"How can you make me feel like this?"

"Like . . . what?"

"Different in a way I have never felt before. You excite me, my darling, but it is much more than that. You are everything I ever wanted in a woman and most of all in my wife."

Then he was kissing her again.

Kissing her so that it was a shock to both of them when the carriage came to a standstill.

They realised they were back at Locke Hall.

Perry was waiting for them.

As they entered the Hall he said teasingly:

"How can you have taken so long?"

Then when Lord Locke would have answered, he said:

"I have given all your orders, so you should be grateful that I managed to get here so quickly."

"I am very grateful," Lord Locke replied, "and now, as we are all hungry, the sooner we have dinner the better!"

He took his evening-cape from around Gytha's shoulders and said:

"If you are going to tidy yourself, please hurry, because we have a lot to celebrate."

She gave him a radiant smile.

Then she ran up the stairs to where Mrs. Meadows was waiting on the landing.

"Whatever happened to you, Miss?" the Housekeeper asked.

"We've all been that worried ever since you was carried off like that!"

"His Lordship rescued me," Gytha replied, "and now everything is wonderful . . . very . . . very . . . wonderful."

She went towards her bedroom as she spoke.

She wanted to hurry back to Lord Locke.

She grudged even the time it took to make herself tidy, when she might have been with him.

They ate a delicious dinner although Gytha had no idea afterwards what she ate or drank.

She could only look at Lord Locke.

It was impossible to believe that he had really said he would marry her.

She thought she must have dreamt it.

All the while Perry was talking and making them laugh she kept meeting Lord Locke's eyes.

It made it impossible to think of anything but his kisses.

Her love seemed to well up inside her, and flow towards him like the rays of the sun.

'No man could be more handsome!' she thought. 'No man could be more attractive or more . . . masculine!'

She blushed at the thought.

It made her look so lovely as she did so that Lord Locke found it difficult to take his eyes from her.

When dinner was over he said gently:

"Go now and get ready, my darling. We are going to be married in the Chapel and my Chaplain is waiting for us."

Gytha drew in her breath.

"Are you . . . quite certain . . . this is what you . . . should do?"

"It is what I am going to do," he replied, "and I will kill anyone who tries to stop me!"

Because of the way he spoke, Gytha felt as if shafts of lightning were seeping through her.

She had no words in which to answer him.

He could see, however, by the expression in her eyes what he had made her feel.

Then without saying any more she ran up the stairs to her bedroom.

Mrs. Meadows was waiting for her.

On the bed was a lace veil that had been in the Locke family for centuries.

Of the finest lace, it might have been made by fairy fingers.

Mrs. Meadows arranged it on her hair.

It fell over her shoulders to the ground and flowed out behind her.

There was a diamond tiara.

Mrs. Meadows told her it had been worn by Lord Locke's great-grandmother.

Fashioned of stars, Gytha thought it might have fallen from the sky especially for her.

Also waiting for her was a small bouquet of orchids.

When she was ready Mrs. Meadows and two housemaids who had come to admire her told her how beautiful she looked.

They wished her luck.

She went down the stairs to where Lord Locke was waiting.

It was difficult to descend slowly.

She wanted to run down to him, but she managed it.

As he met her at the foot of the stairs she realised how magnificent he looked.

He had changed into knee-breeches and silk stockings.

He was also wearing his decorations on his long-tailed coat.

The cross which he had been awarded for gallantry was on a ribbon round his neck.

He took her hand in his.

As he felt her fingers quiver he said in a quiet voice:

"You look exactly as I wanted you to, and when we are married, I will tell you how much I love you."

She drew in her breath.

It was impossible because of her happiness to speak.

He gave her his arm and covered her hand with his.

They walked down the passage towards the Chapel. It was at the back of the house and very old.

It had been built when the foundations of Locke Hall were first laid.

There was the sound of the organ playing before they reached it.

They entered the small Chapel.

Gytha realised that while they were having dinner a profusion of flowers had been arranged on the Altar.

There were also flowers on the sills of the stained-glass windows.

She learnt later that the hot-houses had been emptied.

Every vase of flowers that had been arranged in the house had also been carried to the Chapel.

The air was filled with the fragrance of them.

Instead of the conventional white lilies and carnations there was a mass of colour.

From dahlias and early chrysanthemums as well as orchids and many other hot-house flowers.

Perry was, of course, Lord Locke's Best Man.

The Chaplain, a grey-haired man, began the Service.

Gytha remembered how only a few hours ago she had heard the same opening words.

She had thought they were a death-blow to her happiness and perhaps her life.

Now she was marrying the man she loved and who loved her.

God would bless them and she felt, too, that her mother and father were near her.

They were part of her happiness.

Lord Locke made his responses in a deep, sincere voice.

It made the tears prick Gytha's eyes.

She had admired him from afar for so many years, when he was out riding or hunting.

She knew now that while she admired him for his magnificence, there was also something spiritual about him.

It drew her soul from her body and made it his.

"He is different from all other men," she told herself.

She thanked God that she had found him.

When the Service was over, Lord Locke took Gytha from the Chapel.

She supposed now they would receive the congratulations of the staff.

They would drink a glass of champagne with Perry and the Chaplain.

However, to her surprise, there were no servants in the Hall.

Lord Locke took her upstairs and along a silent corridor to her bedroom.

The lights were burning by the bed.

There was no one in the room.

She looked around her in surprise as he shut the door behind him.

Then he said:

"I want you to myself. We have had more than enough of talking and coping with other people. But now, my darling, we are alone."

She wanted him to kiss her.

But first he lifted the diamond tiara from her hair and took off her veil.

He threw it down on a chair.

Then he pulled her into his arms.

As he kissed her she thought that this was different from the kisses he had given her before.

Now there was something reverent and sacred in it; the Service in which they had just taken was still in both their minds.

As if he were afraid to frighten her, very gently he undid the buttons at the back of her gown.

It slithered like a sigh to the floor.

Gytha felt herself trembling, but not with fear.

An excitement which was a rapture was rising within her.

It was moving like sunshine through her breasts and up into her throat.

It touched her lips that were still held by Lord Locke's.

He lifted her into the bed and laid her back against the pillows.

She felt her heart beating frantically.

There was an ecstasy in her breasts which seemed to grow more and more intense.

A few seconds later Lord Locke joined her.

He put his arms around her.

Then as she felt as if her body melted into his, he asked:

"Now, my precious little wife, I can tell you how much I love you."

"I am . . . dreaming . . . I know I am dreaming!" Gytha cried. "I have . . . loved you for so many years but . . . I never thought . . . that I would ever . . . know you . . . and when I did . . . I never imagined it would be . . . possible for you to . . . love me."

"I love you, for I know that you are what I have been seeking all my life, and thought I would never find."

His lips moved over the softness of her skin as he added:

"At the same time, my precious, if you want me to wait before I make you mine completely and absolutely, so that we are not two people but one, I will do so, although it will be very hard for me."

Gytha gave a little laugh.

Then she hid her face against his neck.

"How can you . . . imagine that I would . . . want to

163

". . . wait for your . . . love?" she asked. "I have waited so long . . . already . . . and when today I thought I had . . . lost you for ever . . . the whole world was . . . dark and empty."

She paused to smile at him lovingly before she added:

"I knew . . . that I had no wish to . . . live if I could not see you."

"That is what I wanted you to say," Lord Locke said. "I want your love, I want it desperately."

His hand touched her hair.

"My precious, I will try to make up to you not only for everything you have suffered this past week, but also for the years with your grandfather and for the loss of your father."

Gytha drew in her breath.

"How can you . . . think of such . . . marvellous . . . fantastic things to say to me?"

"I have known ever since you came to me," Lord Locke replied, "that I had to protect you and to repay the debt I owed your father."

His voice deepened.

"Then because you were so pathetic and at the same time so brave, I fell in love."

Gytha made a little murmur and he said:

"That is true! I know of no woman who would have behaved as you have done in such terrifying and horrible circumstances."

His lips moved over the softness of her cheeks and he went on:

"You are very beautiful, my darling, but I adore your character, besides being overwhelmed by your personality. How can you have so much in one small person?"

"I want to be . . . everything you . . . want me to be,"

Gytha answered, "so will you . . . please . . . teach me how to . . . love you so that . . . I make you really . . . happy and not do anything that you . . . dislike or makes you . . . angry?"

"I have sworn not only to protect you," Lord Locke replied, "but to worship and adore you for as long as we both shall live."

Then he was kissing her, kissing her demandingly.

It was as if he asked something of her.

She was not quite certain what it was.

Yet she wanted to give him herself.

Instinctively she moved closer and still closer to him until she could feel his heart beating against hers.

She knew she had excited him.

There was a fire burning fiercely in his kisses.

She could feel her whole body responding to him.

Little flames flickered through her.

They made her think that the sunshine and lightning were moving together in her body.

Then up into her lips.

"I . . . I love you . . . I love . . . you!"

He was kissing her eyes, her neck, and her breasts.

An ecstasy she had never dreamt possible was a blazing light.

It was so perfect and so glorious.

It could have come only from God.

"I love . . . you with all . . . of me," she murmured aloud.

"I worship you," he answered, "my precious, perfect little wife, but I want you as a woman. Oh, God, I want you!"

Lord Locke made her his.

They became one person and Gytha knew that this was the love of which she had dreamt.

Only, it was far more wonderful.

Far more miraculous than she could ever have imagined.

It was the Glory and Blessing of God.

He had saved them from evil and protected them.

He had given them the true love which was good and pure.

It was theirs now—and for all Eternity.

ABOUT THE AUTHOR

Barbara Cartland, the world's most famous romantic novelist, who is also an historian, playwright, lecturer, political speaker and television personality, has now written over 440 books and sold over 400 million books the world over.

She has also had many historical works published and has written four autobiographies as well as the biographies of her mother and that of her brother, Ronald Cartland, who was the first Member of Parliament to be killed in the last war. This book has a preface by Sir Winston Churchill and has just been republished with an introduction by Sir Arthur Bryant.

Love at the Helm, a novel written with the help and inspiration of the late Admiral of the Fleet, the Earl Mountbatten of Burma, is being sold for the Mountbatten Memorial Trust.

Miss Cartland in 1978 sang an Album of Love Songs with the Royal Philharmonic Orchestra.

In 1976 by writing twenty-one books, she broke the world record and has continued for the following eight years with twenty-four, twenty, twenty-three, twenty-four, twenty-four, twenty-five, twenty-three, and twenty-six. She is in the *Guinness Book of Records* as the best-selling author in the world.

She is unique in that she was one and two in the

Dalton List of Best Sellers, and one week had four books in the top twenty.

In private life Barbara Cartland, who is a Dame of the Order of St. John of Jerusalem, Chairman of the St. John Council in Hertfordshire and Deputy President of the St. John Ambulance Brigade, has also fought for better conditions and salaries for Midwives and Nurses.

Barbara Cartland is deeply interested in Vitamin Therapy and is President of the British National Association for Health. Her book *The Magic of Honey* has sold throughout the world and is translated into many languages. Her designs "Decorating with Love" are being sold all over the U.S.A., and the National Home Fashions League named her in 1981, "Woman of Achievement."

In 1984 she received at Kennedy Airport America's Bishop Wright Air Industry Award for her contribution to the development of aviation; in 1931 she and two R.A.F. Officers thought of, and carried, the first aeroplane-towed glider air-mail.

Barbara Cartland's Romances (a book of cartoons) has been published in Great Britain and the U.S.A., as well as a cookery book, *The Romance of Food*, and *Getting Older, Growing Younger*. She has recently written a children's pop-up picture book, entitled *Princess to the Rescue*.